Foreweird

In a front room bar north of Melbourne's CBD, three local comic creators sit huddled around a bowl of freshly-made potato wedges. Off to the side like naughty schoolkids about to be sent in to the principal's office, we have just made our *entrée* into Melbourne's swarthy comics scene. Various local denizens abound, showing off their latest printed creations amid the beer glasses and smartphones.

With only one self-published book, I'm the only newbie of the three. The other two, however, are Steve Carter and Antoinette Rydyr, a comics duo who have been writing and drawing their own stories for at least a couple of decades. Out of a backpack they slide an A4 display book, with nothing on the cover but a price sticker. Inside, however, are pages and pages of colour printouts of their work, with all manner of malformed monsters, decaying sci-fi beings and human bodies with animal heads. These creatures roam primeval jungles, ancient ruins and futuristic cities. There are exploding skulls, ritual killings, bullets ripping through internal organs, and even a guy who's had a spear thrown through his oldfella. Nice.

Over on a nearby table, some rope-haired dude is pulling out his vast collection of dog-eared graphic novels. They include the sort that contain endless scenes of tightly-rendered muscle men gritting their teeth and bargain-basement dialogue that consists almost entirely of movie trailer quotes; the sort that involve self-insertion characters punching each other (and who ride totally bitchin' 'Hardly-Davidsons' and stuff); and the sort where elves and goblins cavort in a medieval folktale setting — but yet talk like stereotypical jaded '90s slackers.

SCAR care nothing for such pap. The imagery of their comics is unmistakable. Yet this is the same reason why some people seem to writhe in abject fear when looking through their books. Perhaps they won't even get past looking at the cover, and if they don't, what of it?

By now, I've come to know a bit more about how SCAR operate. Sex and violence — to be said in an ominous deep voice — in comics has been criticized ever since the first pen-pusher started drawing the damn things. Over the years, Steve and Antoinette have faced any criticism you care to name. These criticisms affect them deeply, and they take them on board so as not to have to endure them in the future.

Ha! Do they bollocks. Anyone who tells them they suck is summarily ignored, and can go piss up the taps in the boys' dunnies after school. But the funny thing is, most of the finger-wagging comes from people who know nothing about SCAR's comics in the first place. Like the person who told them monsters were evil, then decided to buy a pile of comics before changing their mind. Or the person who didn't know if she was allowed to like their art because she couldn't tell if it was sexist or not.

Or their banning from a comics event for not doing "family friendly" art. Of course it's "family friendly" – if you belong to the Manson Family!

Such deluded individuals clearly don't read SCAR's stuff. Fine! They sure won't be losing any sleep over it. But *you* clearly do – you came here for weirdness, otherworldiness, and maybe even a bit of the old ultra-violence – and that's what you'll get. But don't say you weren't given fair warning!

Some comics writers are content to merely re-hash worlds, giving a warmly deceptive sheen to the reality that somehow resembles our own. Not SCAR. They want to create their own worlds; new ones that they have imagined, dreamed up over long brainstorming sessions and lengthy viewings of pop-cultural flotsam from yesteryear, inspired by the devolved monster un-creations that have been spewed up from the earth's scarred bowels, and stirred up by their long-held fascination with the most primitive and brutal of ancient civilizations.

The worlds you are about to encounter in the following pages are far removed from the deadbeat everyday Australian suburbia that the comics creators inhabit as they mingle around the barroom tables. These are worlds where you are just as likely to encounter 'Torso Boy' twitching spastically on the floor of a speeding bus, as you are to witness the gleaming white edifices of Perfectown. You may not be ready for what's about to transpire in these grim locales, but nobody ever said that these journeys would be easy. And, shock horror, as one of my teachers used to say – you may learn something.

Still, away with such small talk. It is now time for you to begin your descent into *Weird Worlds*. Because if you don't, you will be forced to endure reading the aforementioned rope-haired dude's ratty comic collection. And I guarantee you, it won't be nearly as satisfyingly grotesque as this.

Pete Correy
December 2016

AUSTRALIA AFTER THE FALL – LIKE THE REST OF THE GLOBE, A LAND BESIEGED BY HIGHLY ADAPTIVE HYBRIDS, EVOLUTIONARY DESCENDANTS OF GENETIC EXPERIMENTS CREATED BY TERRORISTS DURING AN APOCALYPTIC RELIGIOUS WAR – EAST VERSUS WEST – THAT DEVASTATED THE WORLD.
MS FEMISMO
THE PURPOSE OF THESE CREATURES HAD BEEN TO POPULATE THE EARTH WITH THE INFERNAL FAUNA OF HELL AND DESTROY ALL NON-BELIEVERS.
BY STEVE CARTER & ANTOINETTE RYDYR © 2011-12
DAMN YOU, TRAVIS. YOUR HIGH FLYING HAS ATTRACTED SWIPERS!
ZR
RAP!
JUST MY LUCK! – WINDING UP ON MS FEMISMO'S CREW!
COULD THINGS GET ANY WORSE?
HELL YEAH! THEY JUST DID. TRAVIS GOT SWIPED AND THAT BITCH IS PISSED WITH HIM FOR IT!
EMPATHY SURE ISN'T HER STRONG SUIT.
COUNTLESS GENERATIONS LATER, THEY REPRESENTED THE LARGEST, MOST DANGEROUS GROUP OF LIFEFORMS ON THE ENTIRE PLANET.

BECAUSE THEY WERE THE ULTIMATE PRODUCT OF AMBITIOUS RELIGIOUS FANATICS, THE ACTIONS OF WHOM HAD IRREVERSIBLY CHANGED THE WORLD, RELIGIOUS INSTITUTIONS WERE PROHIBITED AND THOSE WHO PRACTICED RELIGION WERE BRANDED AS CRIMINALS.
- AND THEN THERE WAS MS FEMISMO, A HARSH, BRASH BUT ATTRACTIVE AND EFFICIENT WOMAN. SHE HAD TAKEN OUT MORE HYBRIDS THAN ANYONE ELSE. THE DEPARTMENT REGARDED HER AS THEIR BEST ASSET AND PUT HER IN CHARGE OF DEFENCE. SHE SAVED MORE LIVES THAN ANY OTHER CREW MEMBER AND THE MEN FAWNED OVER HER, REGARDLESS OF HER ABRASIVE MANNER.
GET DOWN INTO THAT CANYON, UNDER COVER!
- BEFORE WE ALL DIE UP HERE!
WE HAVE A MISSION TO COMPLETE!
BUT DESPITE MS FEMISMO'S EFFORTS, THERE WERE ALWAYS CASUALTIES. IT CAME WITH THE JOB.
MOST TERRIFYING OF ALL OF THE RAMPAGING GENETIC FREAKS WERE THE HYBRID HUMAN-ANIMALS -
- THE NOTORIOUS GENE SNATCHERS AND WOMB RAIDERS, SPECIALISED ADAPTIVES THAT PREYED ON HUMANS, AND ONE ANOTHER, TO PROPAGATE THEIR EVER-EVOLVING SPECIES.
A MARAUDING BAND OF SATAURS HAD RAIDED ONE OF THE OUTLYING VILLES AND ABDUCTED THREE YOUNG WOMEN...
2

I'VE NOTIFIED BASE OF THE DEATHS OF TWO CREW-MEMBERS IN ACTION.
NOW, WE MUST RESUME OUR SEARCH FOR THE ABDUCTED WOMEN.
SATAURS HAVE HIDDEN DENS THROUGHOUT THIS CANYON. THERE IS ALSO A PROLIFERATION OF CLAM-FACED NYMPHOSAURS DOWN HERE. THEY'RE COMPLETELY INDISCRIMINATE WHEN CHASING MALES TO FERTILISE THEIR EGGS –
REMAIN ALERT AT ALL TIMES!
BITCH!
AS FOR YOU, EVANS!
FLYIN' TOO CLOSE!
SPREAD OUT!
"ON THAT CLIFF! NYMPHOSAURS!"
"UNSIGHTLY LOOKIN' THINGS–"
"YEAH, BUT THEY LIKE THE SIGHT OF YOU BOYS."
"YOU WON'T GET ME WITHIN FIFTY FEET OF THOSE THINGS, MS FEMISMO!"
"OH, COME ON, NOW, AMES!"
3

THE NYMPHOSAURS HAD NO INTEREST IN THE WOMEN;
THE FLESH OF MALES NURTURED FERTILISED EGGS BEST.

JUST ONE OF THE SATAURS
WAS TARGETED BY BOTH
NYMPHOSAURS IN A SAVAGE
BID TO SUBDUE AND MATE
HIM, RESULTING IN AN
ALL-OUT FIGHT FOR LIFE.

BEFORE THE
ASTOUNDED AND
TERRIFIED GAZE OF
ONE OF THE SATAURS'
CAPTIVES, THE THREE
BATTLING HYBRIDS
TUMBLED OFF THE EDGE
OF A LOFTY PRECIPICE
INTO OBLIVION.

4

AT THE BOTTOM OF THE GORGE A MASSIVE NAMELESS MUTANT FEASTED ON THE DEAD.
DOWN THERE, MS!
WE SHOULD RUN!
NOWHERE TO RUN.
STAY HERE, WE'RE DEAD OR WORSE!
NOW THAT ONE OF THEM HAD BEEN SLAIN, THE REMAINING PAIR OF SATAURS VICIOUSLY FOUGHT OVER WHICH OF THEM WAS GOING TO LAY CLAIM ON THE DEAD ONE'S WOMAN. IT WAS DURING THE HEAT OF THIS CONFLICT THAT THE SEARCH PARTY CAME UPON THEM,

THE SATAURS INSTANTLY FLED IN OPPOSITE DIRECTIONS.
THIS REQUIRES PRECISION SHOOTING! HIT ONE OF THOSE GIRLS, YOU'LL INCUR A COURT MARTIAL!
F-FOOP
F-H-
P-TANG!
F-ZUP!
?!
BOTH OF THEM ARE WOUNDED AND BLEEDING; THEY'LL BE EASY TO TRACK. AMES, YOU PAIR WITH DELVINE, OUR NEW RECRUIT. MACY, EVANS AND NEL – TEND TO THE WOMEN UNTIL MEDVAC ARRIVES.
MURPHY, YOU'RE WITH ME, TRACKING THE OTHER SATAUR.
YES, MS.
SHE'S LED HIM UP HERE, TO THOSE CAVES.
THIS'S CLOSE ENOUGH. WE GO IN ON FOOT.
IT IS ESSENTIAL WE MAINTAIN THE ELEMENT OF SURPRISE.
THEY'RE CERTAINLY NOT AFTER THAT SATAUR, TOO HIGH UP!

BE VERY CAUTIOUS, KEEP YOUR WEAPON READY!
I'VE LOST DELVINE AND AMES' SIGNAL, BUT THEY'VE GOT TO BE CLOSE.
THERE'S A REASON I HAD DELVINE TRANSFERRED TO THIS CREW. LAST THREE MEN WHO DISAPPEARED WERE LAST SEEN WITH HER.
THIS IS WHERE THE LAST OF THE NYMPHILIUM FLED OVER A DECADE AGO, SUPPOSED LOCATION OF THEIR TEMPLE. SHE WAS NEVER FOUND!
DO YOU TRULY BELIEVE DELVINE IS THE LAST OF...
MORE LIKELY SHE'S A DESCENDANT, AND I'VE SEEN NYMPHILIUM LARVAE FLYING THROUGHOUT THE REGION.
ARE YOU CERTAIN, AND COULD THEY BE OF THE SAME BROOD?
I'VE SEEN THEM, AND IF THEY ARE ALL OF THE SAME MATERNAL LINE,
- AND IF SHE'S DUE TO TRANSMORPH INTO A QUEEN!
- A NYMPHILIUM QUEEN, THE SUPREME WARRIOR FORM, CAPABLE OF PRODUCING PRODIGOUS NUMBERS,
I KNOW THE LEGEND, AND THE ASPIRATION OF EVERY NYMPHILIUM - TO CREATE AN INVINCIBLE ARMY OF NYMPHILIUM QUEENS DESCENDED FROM ONE MATERNAL LINE!
SEVERAL MINDS WORKING AS ONE! A HIVE MIND HELL-BENT ON WORLD DOMINATION.
ALL NYMPHILIUM WORSHIP THEIR QUEENS AS GODDESSES. IT IS THEIR RELIGION!
NOT FAR AWAY, WITHIN A VAST CAVERN,
SO, AMES, YOU WERE THE BAIT AND MS FEMISMO THE SNARE!
THOUGHT YOU'D TRAP ME AND FIND MY LAIR...
NEVER UNDERESTIMATE THE POWER OF RELIGION, MURPHY, IT COMES IN MANY INSIDIOUS FORMS AND WAS USED TO CREATE THE WORLD WE LIVE IN TODAY.
BY THE TIME SHE GETS HERE, I'LL HAVE BECOME A QUEEN, LOVER BOY!
C'MON. YOU KNOW WHAT TO DO; SHE CAN'T HELP YOU.
OH, YES! C'MON! LET IT COME!

NYMPHILIUM LARVAE! INSIDIOUS, VILE LITTLE SCRAGLETS!
VERY RECENT HATCHLINGS, JUDGING BY THE SIZE OF THEM!
ACCURSED THINGS ARE SWARMIN'!
ALL THEY DO IS RAPACIOUSLY FEED AND CHASE ANYTHING MALE.
VERY FEW OF THEM BECOME NYMPHILIUM.
THEY NEVER GET ENOUGH SEX AND CANNOT MORPH!
THIS LOT ARE NEVER GONNA GET THE CHANCE, THAT'S A PROMISE!

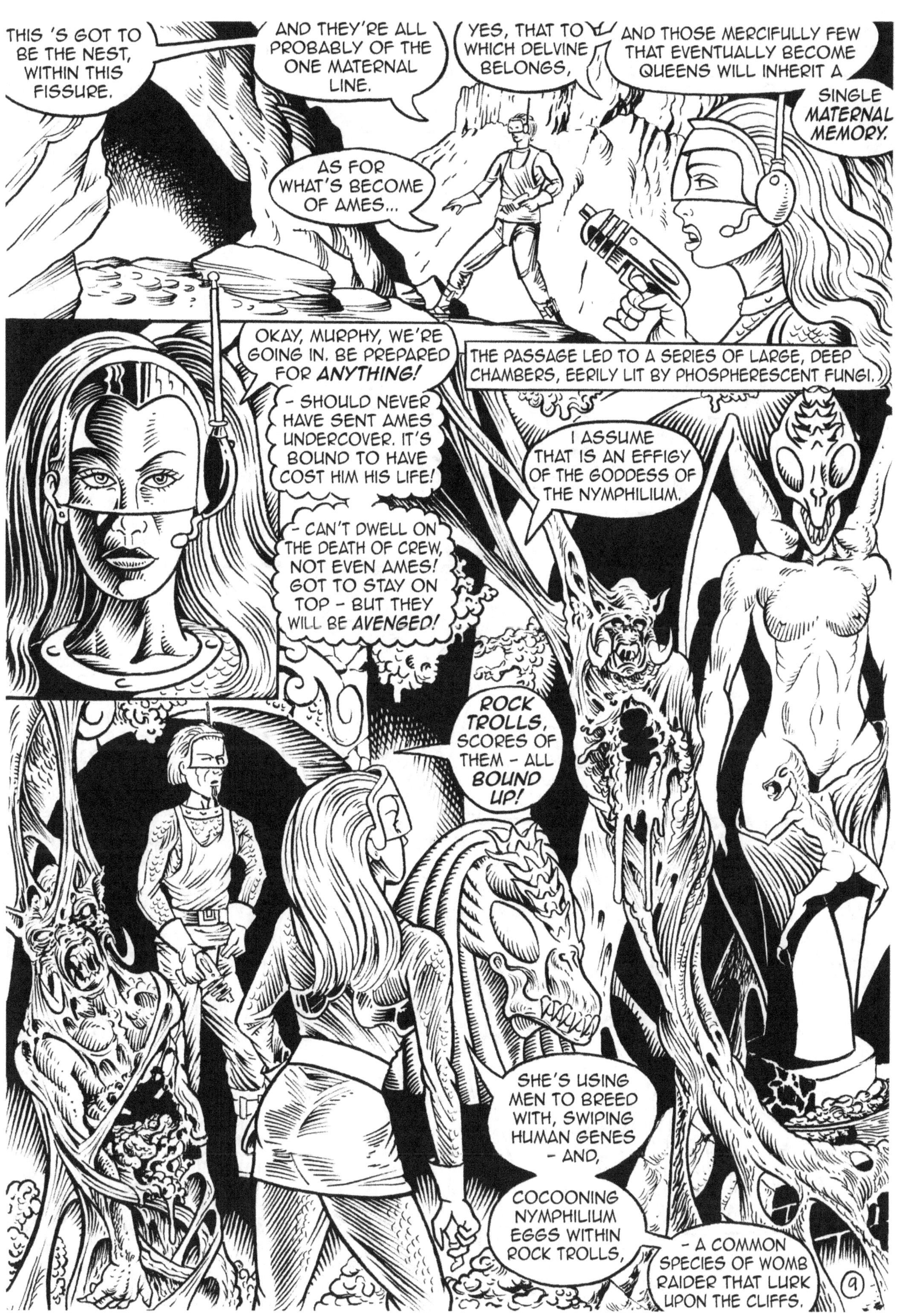

THIS 'S GOT TO BE THE NEST, WITHIN THIS FISSURE.

AND THEY'RE ALL PROBABLY OF THE ONE MATERNAL LINE.

YES, THAT TO WHICH DELVINE BELONGS,

AND THOSE MERCIFULLY FEW THAT EVENTUALLY BECOME QUEENS WILL INHERIT A SINGLE MATERNAL MEMORY.

AS FOR WHAT'S BECOME OF AMES...

OKAY, MURPHY, WE'RE GOING IN. BE PREPARED FOR ANYTHING!

- SHOULD NEVER HAVE SENT AMES UNDERCOVER. IT'S BOUND TO HAVE COST HIM HIS LIFE!

- CAN'T DWELL ON THE DEATH OF CREW, NOT EVEN AMES! GOT TO STAY ON TOP - BUT THEY WILL BE AVENGED!

THE PASSAGE LED TO A SERIES OF LARGE, DEEP CHAMBERS, EERILY LIT BY PHOSPHERESCENT FUNGI.

I ASSUME THAT IS AN EFFIGY OF THE GODDESS OF THE NYMPHILIUM.

ROCK TROLLS, SCORES OF THEM - ALL BOUND UP!

SHE'S USING MEN TO BREED WITH, SWIPING HUMAN GENES - AND,

COCOONING NYMPHILIUM EGGS WITHIN ROCK TROLLS,

- A COMMON SPECIES OF WOMB RAIDER THAT LURK UPON THE CLIFFS.

I HAVE TAKEN COUNTLESS LOVERS FROM YOUR MIDST, AND THEY WERE HAPPY TO INDULGE ME, EXCEPT FOR A FEW, LIKE YOU!
YEAH, RIGHT!
YOU CONSPIRED WITH THAT MACHISMO BITCH TO COMMIT GENOCIDE UPON MY KIND, AND FOR THAT, YOU WILL PAY. HAD YOU BEEN CONTENT TO SIMPLY BE MY LOVER, I'D HAVE SET YOU FREE.
IT IS THE LESSER BRUTES THAT WE USE TO GESTATE OUR EGGS, BUT THIS LAST BATCH IS OF GREAT SIGNIFICANCE,
IT IS THE ONE THAT WILL SEE ME ASCEND TO A QUEEN.
- WHAT BETTER MAN IS THERE BUT YOU TO SERVE AS THEIR RECEPTACLE AND INCUBATOR. JUST RELAX, NOW SWALLOW!
I AM ONE,
AND I AM MANY!
I AM AT ONCE A WARRIOR,
A GODDESS AND ALL NYMPHILIUM!
I AM THE NYMPHILIUM QUEEN; MY DUTY IS TO DESTROY ALL WHO INTEND TO HARM NYMPHILIUM.
...WAIT! I HEAR THEM! INTRUDERS!
10

DELVINE, NOT YET WHOLLY TRANSFORMED INTO A NYMPHILIUM QHEEN, RACED FROM THE CAVERNOUS BOWELS OF THE TEMPLE INTO THE UPPER TIERS, WHERE SHE CAME UPON MURPHY, WHO SHE QUICKLY OVERPOWERED. SHE SAW NO SIGN OF MS FEMISMO...
BEFORE YOU WAGED WAR WITH US, WITH ME, NYMPHILIUM NEVER HARMED ANY HUMAN! HUMANITY PLAYS A VITAL ROLE IN OUR EVOLUTION.
NOW, I CAN CREATE SCIONS OF NEW NYMPHILIUM FROM A SINGLE UNION WITH ONE MAN - I HAVE JUST DONE SO USING AMES!
EACH, LIKE ALL OTHERS, ARE VERSIONS OF ME!
THAT'S GOT TO BE DELVINE! THE HAIR, EMERALD EYES! IT'S OBVIOUS!
HASN'T COMPLETED MORPHING, SHE HASN'T SEEN ME - BUT SHE WILL, ANY MOMENT NOW -
NO, THEY DON'T LOOK THE SAME, YOUR HUMAN GENES HAVE ALLOWED FOR INFINITE VARIATIONS AND ADAPTATION.
BUT THEY HAVE MY MEMORY, PERSONALITY, AND NEW SKILLS, MORE KNOWLEDGE!
GO DIE, HYBRID FREAK WHORE!
DIE?
NYMPHILIUM ARE A FORM OF IMMORTALITY! NOW, WE ARE YOUR ENEMY. YOU CANNOT KILL US ALL; THIS IS A WAR YOU WILL NOT WIN!
AND YOU, MURPHY, SPINELESS SYCOPHANT OF THAT WAR-MONGERING BITCH, MS FEMISMO, SHALL BE NEXT TO JOIN MY INFINITE HAREM!
11

AFTER THE DELVINE-HYBRID WAS DISPATCHED AN EXTERMINATION CREW WAS CALLED IN TO CLEAN OUT THE VAST SUBTERRANEAN TEMPLE. AMES UNDERWENT SEVERAL COMPLEX OPERATIONS AND A LENGTHY REHABILITATION PROGRAM, BUT NOT ALL OF DELVINE'S NYMPHILIUM OFFSPRING COULD BE ACCOUNTED FOR. MANY HAD PREVIOUSLY HATCHED AND LEFT THE TEMPLE.

THE FUGLIES
BY S. CARTER & A. RYDYR 2001/14
...IT'S NOT A GOOD IDEA FOR US TO BE SUNBATHING NAKED WAY OUT HERE, GLORIA.
SIGHTINGS OF FUGLIES HAVE BEEN REPORTED...
WE'RE BIG GIRLS, RAE, AND WE CAN TAKE CARE OF OURSELVES.
WE'VE GOT OUR SIDE-ARMS HANDY,
...AND A VERY FAST GET-AWAY VEHICLE...
IT'S 40° PLUS TODAY...
YOU GOING TO STAY OUT THERE WORRYING YOUR LITTLE PIN-HEAD OFF OR...
ARE YOU COMING IN TO COOL OFF?
YEAH, SO?
THOSE CUTE TITSIES OF YOURS'LL BE ROASTED REDDER THAN THEIR CHERRY TIPS!
SHIT
GET OUT OF THE WATER NOW, GLORIA!
...AND GET YOUR SIDE-ARM!
SPREAD OUT, YOU RETARDS! DON'T CROWD ME!
GET 'ROUND THEM! DON'T LET THEM GET TO THAT FLYIN' CAR.
BUT THEY GOT GUNS, MARYLIN!
DON'T LET THAT STOP YOU!
FORGET YOUR CLOTHES! GRAB YOUR GUN AN' HEAD FOR THE GRAVCAR!
...SILLY BITCH! TOLD YOU THERE ARE FUGLIES 'ROUND HERE!
JEZUZ! THEY'RE HUGE!

A DIRECT HIT TO THE HEART IS THE ONLY THING THAT WILL TAKE THEM OUT!
BUT YOU'VE GOT TO CRACK THEIR INCREDIBLY THICK STERNUMS FIRST.
KRAK!
ZRIP!
KTLAK!
GET THAT BITCH, BOY!
FERGIT THAT HAND!
...IT'LL HAVE GROWN BACK BY NEXT SUMMER!
KEEP TRYIN', LIDDLE LADY!
...FER ALL THE GOOD IDD'LE DO YER!
PUT EIGHT ROUNDS IN THIS FREAK'S STERNUM!
SHT!!
FOOMP FOOMP!
FOOMP FOOMP!
AND STILL HAVEN'T SMASHED THROUGH TO ITS HEART!
HEY, TWIGGY GIRL! ...YOU LET THAT PEA-SHOOTER OFF JUS' ONCE MORE, LOBSTER BOY HERE'S GONNA POP YER GIRLFRIEND'S SCRAWNY NECK!
I DROP THIS GUN, WE'VE BOTH HAD IT!

LAST WARNING! DROP THE GUN OR THE BITCH GETS CHILLED.
GLORIA'S BULLETS MADE A MESS OF THIS FREAK'S STERNUM. IT CAN BARELY STAND...
ONE GOOD SHOT SHOULD CRACK IT WIDE OPEN AND DROP HER...
...IS IT WORTH THE RISK?
...NOT THAT THERE'S REALLY A CHOICE...
NIARRGH!
THAK!
KLAM
KNOW WHAT? I THINK YOU'RE BLUFFING!
IMPOSSIBLE! MOTHER MARYLIN HAS BEEN KILLED!
COME BACK, WOMAN! YOU BELONG TO ME!
C'MON, GLORIA! STOP FUCKIN' 'ROUND! RUN!
YOU'RE NOT GONNA GET A SECOND CHANCE!
REMIND ME TO PACK EXPLOSIVE TIPPED ROUNDS NEXT TIME. FUGLY STERNUMS ARE TOUGH!
THANKS, RAE. THOUGHT THAT WAS IT FOR ME...
VVRIIIZZZ!
THAT WAS A DICEY ONE, ALRIGHT!
...BUT I WAS PRETTY SURE THEY WOULDN'T KILL YOU...
THEY WANT US ALIVE, AND YOU KNOW WHY...
SURE DO! ONE OF THE REASONS WHY EVERYONE FINDS FUGLIES SO OBSCENE!

IT'S A MAN OF THE HUMAN CLAN!
SOMEONE ATE HIM!
BET I KNOW WHO!
YOU DON'T KNOW NOTHIN' LOBSTER BOY!
I KNOW NONE OF US ATE HIM...
HE'S NOT BEEN THERE LONG. ...FRESH!
...MISSION ACCOMPLISHED!
TOOK CARE OF TWO THINGS AT ONCE. MORGDRON HAD TO GO AND WE NEEDED SUSTENANCE.
THOSE FUGLIES HADN'T TURNED UP IT'D HAVE BEEN PERFECT!
NO DRAMA NOW, TOOK CARE OF 'EM ANYHOW. AS IT HAPPENS WE CHILLED THEIR LEADER!
...GLAD YOU HAD A SPARE OUTFIT IN THE GLOVE BOX, CAME IN HANDY.
THE SISTERS MAGDAGALA ARE HERE AND THEY'RE NOT PLEASED!
THEY NEVER ARE ...SO WHAT?
BROUGHT IT IN CASE THE BUSINESS WITH MORGDRON GOT MESSY,
...WHICH IT DID.
YOU'VE GOT A HOLSTER, MICRO MINI, HALTER, THE LOT...
MOTHER MARYLIN LIES DEAD!
...YOU LET TWO PERFECTLY GOOD INCUBATORS ESCAPE!
INCOMPETANT CRETINS, ALL OF YOU!!
...TURNS OUT, YOU NEED THEM, ALONG WITH THAT ID CHIP.
...WON'T GET THROUGH ANY ENTRY PORT BACK AT PERFECTOWN WITHOUT THEM ~ AS YOU KNOW.

SHIT! IT'S PRACTICALLY CURFEW TIME!
...HAVE TO HURRY! THIS BUG'S NOT BACK BY CURFEW, HIRE COMPANY'LL REPORT IT STOLEN!
SO WHAT? HIRED IT WITH A FAKE ID...
...DIDN'T YOU...?
ER, YEAH, AS ALWAYS.
BUT I HAD TO FRONT A LARGE BOND.
TRANSCITY ATMOSPHERIC FILTERING AND PURIFICATION
CURRENT PERMIT REQUIRED
ENTRY PORT
STOP
STOP
SURCHARGE APPLIES
HAD TO USE CASH OR THEY WOULDN'T GIVE ME THE GRAVCAR.
SHIT!
...I INTEND TO COLLECT...
WELCOME TO THE CITY OF PERFECTOWN
COMPLETELY POLLUTION FREE, FULLY ENCLOSED ATMOSPHERE, YOUR HEALTH IS OUR PRIORITY!
MOTHER MARYLIN IS GONE. WE ARE NEXT IN LINE. FROM NOW ON, YOU WILL ALL REFER TO US AS THE MOTHERS MAGDAGALA ...ANY OBJECTIONS?
THE MOTHERS MAGDAGALA ARE OUR CLAN MATRONS.
SEE THAT YOU DO!
WE WILL OBEY THEIR EVERY COMMAND.
NOW, WE SHALL HONOUR MOTHER MARYLIN'S UNTIMELY PASSING. REMEMBER HER WISE WORDS, WHICH ARE THOSE OF ALL GREAT CLAN MATRONS!
ALL FLESH IS MEAT. WASTE NOT, WANT NOT. TO EAT IS TO REGENERATE!
WHAT'S KEEPING THEM? SHOULD HAVE LET US STRAIGHT THROUGH...
...PASS IS VALID, ISN'T IT?
SURE IS, BUT YOU HEARD 'IM...
...A HOLD UP WITH PROCESIN' OR SOME SUCH...
YEAH, RIGHT!

THAT'S THEM, ALL RIGHT! THANKS FOR ALERTING US, GOOD WORK. NOW, JUST KEEP STALLING THEM...
WE'RE ALMOST THERE.
NEEDLESS TO SAY, THEY'RE ARMED AND FLAUNTING IT. DON'T DROP YOUR GUARD FOR A MOMENT! THESE TWO ARE PHASE TWO REGENS.
I KNOW. DEALT WITH PLENTY OF THEM AND THEY'RE ALL PSYCHO!
...WORSE THAN PHASE ONES ~ FUGLIES. ...AND JUST AS HARD TO TAKE OUT...
MY FEELINGS EXACTLY...
OKAY, WE KNOW THEY ABDUCTED PROFESSOR MORGDRON MY GUESS IS THAT HIS BODY'S OUT THERE SOMEWHERE - WHAT'S LEFT OF IT, THAT IS...
SHIT!
HOLD TIGHT, GLORIA. WE'RE LEAVING, AND FAST!
PUT'CHA FOOT DOWN, RAE. THEY'RE RIGHT UP OUR ARSE!
DOIN' THE BEST I CAN ~ IT'S ONLY A SHITBOX HIRE-CAR.
OH MI GORD! WHERE DID THAT COME FROM?
NOWHERE I SWEAR!
JEZUZ SHIT!
JUS' KNEW THEY'D DO A RUNNER!
K'NEL!
THE SKY'S ANARCHY! GET ME BACK ON THE GROUND, NOW!
GLORIA! SIT BACK DOWN, CRAZY BITCH! NO POINT! VEHICLE'S IMPERVIOUS TO BULLETS. SAVE IT!
K'RUK!
HUH?
WHO THE HELL ARE THEY, WHAT DO THEY WANT?
YOU SHOULD KNOW!
IT'S THAT NOSY SLUT WHO'S BEEN INVESTIGATIN' LOCAL ILLICIT REGEN OPERATIONS.
...AND SHE OBVIOUSLY WANTS US!
MOMENTS LATER, THE WILD CHASE HAD LED THEM FROM THE CONGESTED AIRWAYS AROUND THE CITY BACK OUT OVER THE WILDERNESS...
GOT THEM!
THEY'VE PUT A TRACTOR BEAM ON US!
WHAT JUST HAPPENED?
WE'LL NEVER BREAK OUT OF THAT! NOT WITH THIS LITTLE SHITBOX, IT'S GUTLESS!
...GOT AN IDEA. GET THE PORTABLE GRAV DISCS OUT OF THE GLOVE BOX. PUT ONE ON AND GIVE THE OTHER TO ME ...QUICKLY!

PLEASE DON'T THINK I'M UNGRATEFUL, MOTHERS MAGDAGALA, BUT YOU LET THOSE TWO HAVE MORE MEAT THAN ANY OF US. THEY HAD OVER HALF OF MOTHER MARYLIN BETWEEN THEM!
THEY NEED IT, LOBSTERBOY. SINCE THE DAY THEY WERE BEHEADED IN THAT FIGHT WITH THE MEGAERA CLAN THEY'VE HAD TO GROW NEW HEADS AND BRAINS. THEY BARELY HAVE A NEW SET OF EYES, MOUTHS AND EARS, YET!
AND BEFORE YOU ASK - NO, THEY WON'T BE ABLE TO REMEMBER WHO THEY WERE...
THEY'LL HAVE TO LEARN EVERYTHING AGAIN!
THAT'S THEIR FLYIN' CAR! ...THE BITCHES THAT KILLED MOTHER MARYLIN!
YOU SURE LOBSTER BOY?
OR ARE YOU JUS' BABBLIN' LIKE YOU DO?
IT'S THEM!
THAT'S IT...
WE'RE BAILIN'. MAKE SURE YOU ACTIVATE YOUR PORTABLE GRAV DISC.
IT'S ON!
GOOD. SLAMMIN' THIS CRATE IN HARD REVERSE SHOULD FUCK 'EM UP GOOD!
NOW, JUMP!
I WAS EXPECTIN' SOMETHIN' LIKE THIS FROM THOSE TWO!
CUT THE TRACTOR BEAM NOW!
WON'T WORK!
...HOPE YOU'RE WEARIN' YOUR GRAVDISC...
ALWAYS.
ACTIVATE IT!
JUST DID!
HERE WE GO, READY OR NOT!
EJECT!
VRUUSH!
KBOOM!
SHIT!

NEVER USED A PORTABLE GRAV DISC BEFORE...
IT'S FREAKY!
...CAN'T TELL IF I'M FALLING OR FLOATING...
YOU'LL BE FINE, GLORIA!
YOU MIGHT NOT BE ABLE TO FLY WITH THESE...
BUT YOU'LL DEFINITELY HAVE A SOFT LANDING.
MOMENTS LATER AND NOT FAR AWAY...
YOU OKAY, MASON?
I'LL LIVE.
GOOD. GOT TO STAY RIGHT ON THOSE TWO REGEN SLAGS. CAN'T HAVE THEM SLIP AWAY NOW!
...REPORTS SAY FUGLIES HAVE BEEN SIGHTED HERE...
NO PROBLEM. WE'VE GOT PLENTY OF EXPLOSIVE ROUNDS.
...BRING 'EM ON!
THEY WENT DOWN OVER THERE!
THAT'S MOTHER MEGAERA'S TERRITORY.
YES, IT IS! ...AND WE'RE AT WAR WITH HER CLAN.
NO MATTER. WE'RE GOING OVER THERE TO GET THOSE BITCHES!
THAT PAIR BAILED WITH SECONDS TO SPARE, I'M TRULY SORRY TO SAY...
THIS IS LOOKIN' BAD.
IF THAT BITCH'S WHO I THINK SHE IS...
...AND I'M SURE IT'S HER...
...USED TO BE A CULLER, BACK BEFORE IT WAS ABOLISHED...
WORD IS, SHE'S KILLED HUNDREDS OF REGENS,
...PHASE TWOS AS WELL AS FUGLIES.
SHE'S NOT GOING TO STOP UNTIL SHE'S GOT US...

YOU TELLIN' ME THAT SLUT IS UNA KOSCHE?
I'VE HEARD OF HER. WHO HASN'T?
IT'S GOT TO BE HER. THE LATEST IS THAT SHE'S A HIGH RANKIN' REGULATOR.
THEY WOULDN'T HAVE HER! SHE'S A MANIAC WITH AN AMBITION TO EXTERMINATE ALL REGENS!
...SO SAYS THE URBAN MYTH. ...HER DARLING BROTHER WAS EATEN ALIVE BY PHASE TWOS ~ LIKE US ~ WHEN SHE WAS A CHILD...
IT WAS ALL OVER THE MEDIA AT THE TIME.
NOW, SHE'S HITTIN' ALL THE ILLICIT REGEN OPS.
YEAH? WELL, FUCK HER!
RATBATS!
SOMETHING STARTLED THEM.
BRIP!
BRIP!
BRIP!
BRIP!
...IT CAME OUT OF NOWHERE!
...AND JUST AS SUDDENLY DISAPPEARED!
...OBVIOUSLY THE PROGENY OF THE VERY FIRST REGEN PROGRAMS. ...BUT INSTEAD OF PRODUCING LIVESTOCK THAT REGENERATED LIMBS, THUS GIVING US AN ENDLESS SUPPLY OF MEAT...
...THEY CREATED A BREED OF UNCONTROLLABLE, HIDEOUS FREAKS!
AND THINGS PROCEEDED TO GO DOWNHILL FROM THAT POINT ON. THIS WHOLE REGEN SHIT IS GOING TO GO DOWN AS THE BIGGEST HUMAN FOLLY OF ALL...
NOW, THAT THING WAS PARALYSED WITH FEAR,
...AND WHATEVER IT WAS FLEEING FROM HAS GOT TO BE CLOSE...
RRRAAAGH!
?
!?

SCANT SECONDS LATER THEY WERE SURROUNDED!
...AS THE MELEE INTENSIFIED, A HUGE CYCLOPEAN BEING WATCHED FROM THE SAFETY OF A HIGH, ROCKY BLUFF. HER NAME WAS MOTHER MEGAERA, THE CLAN'S MATRON...
KOOM!
THAK
S. CARTER © 2003

HEAR THAT, RAE? THAT'S ONE HELL OF A SHITFIGHT GOING ON BACK THERE!
NO WAY WE'RE GONNA BE PART OF IT. C'MON, MOVE YOUR ARSE!
...SHOULD MAKE IT TO TRASHTOWN BY NIGHTFALL ...IT'S NOT FAR FROM HERE.
WHAT'S AT TRASHTOWN THAT COULD POSSIBLY HELP US?
...SHIT IT'S HOT OUT HERE!
MORE OF OUR KIND FOR ONE THING...
...NOT TO MENTION AMMO, WHICH WE NEED MORE OF,
...AND LAST BUT NOT LEAST, SHELTER AND SOME PLACE TO HIDEOUT.
THOSE TWO ARE DOING PLENTY OF DAMAGE!
MOST OF THE CLAN WILL RECOVER, REGENERATE.
BUT CATERPILLAR MAN AND ONE OF THE HUMAN HAMMERHEAD TWINS ARE DEAD!
BUT WE'VE FINALLY TRAPPED THAT PAIR NOW! THEY'VE GOT NOWHERE TO RUN!
THAT CLIFF IS A HUNDRED FEET HIGH!
...I'LL HAVE THE MAN. THAT FEISTY BITCH WILL BE SEEDED BY THE CLAN'S MALES - ALL OF THEM!
ON THE COUNT OF TWO.
...WE TURN AND JUMP!
READY WHEN YOU ARE...

KHOOOM!!
OBLITERATED IT'S HEAD. WHAT A MESS!
IT'LL SURVIVE.
THAT'S A PITY!
...I'VE SEEN A NEW SET OF JAWS GROW INSIDE THE CARNAGE OF THE SEVERED NECK OF A FUGLY WITHIN EIGHT HOURS OF IT BEING DECAPPED.
...DOESN'T SURPRISE ME. NO DOUBT, IT SPROUTED A BRAND NEW HEAD AND BRAIN AFTER A WEEK.
YEAH, PRETTY MUCH.
...REALLY IS TIME TO CALL FOR BACK-UP, NOW. VEHICLE'S TOTALLED, WE'RE OUTNUMBERED...
WE'LL BE FINE.
I ADMIRE YOUR CONFIDENCE AND COURAGE BUT...
WE'RE FINISHING WHAT WE CAME HERE FOR.
IT'S OUR JOB, NOBODY ELSE'S...
WHAT YOU REALLY MEAN IS THAT YOU WANT THOSE TWO PHASE TWOS ALL TO YOURSELF. THIS IS PERSONAL, ISN'T IT?
IT'S OUR CASE, THEREFORE, IT'S OUR DUTY. NOTHING MORE.
EVEN SO, SOME BACK-UP'D TIP THE ODDS IN OUR FAVOUR. WE COULD USE IT.
WE ALREADY HAVE ALL THE ADVANTAGE WE NEED...
...CLEARLY FUNCTIONING BRAINS...
...NOT TO MENTION OUR FIREPOWER
I HOPE YOU'RE RIGHT...
12

THE BIG ATTRACTOR IS THE *ETERNAL YOUTH AND BEAUTY MYTH*, A SHORT-CUT TO *IMMORTALITY*. YOUNG GIRLS TAKE TO THE PHASE TWO PROCESS BETTER THAN ANYONE ELSE. IT'S SOMEHOW LINKED TO HORMONES. THE UPSHOT IS THAT ANY AND *ALL* DAMAGED CELLS CAN REGENERATE BUT AS IN ALL REGENS, JUST LIKE THE *FUGLIES*, IT TAKES A MASSIVE INTAKE OF *FLESH* TO FUEL IT...

"...THEIR METABOLISM, PHYSIOLOGY AND PSYCHOLOGICAL PROCESSES ADJUST ACCORDINGLY, TURNING THEM *HYPER-PREDATORY*, AND THEIR AGGRESSION RISES TO A PSYCHOPATHIC LEVEL. THEY BECOME COMPLETELY UNCONTROLLABLE. IN ORDER TO SATIATE THEIR *NEEDS* THEY'LL COMMIT APPALLING CRIMES. THOSE TWO ARE IMPLICATED IN ACTS OF *CANNIBALISM*."

YES, THE GRUESOME DEATH OF MANUEL FERGUSON COMES TO MIND. IT OCCURRED AROUND A WEEK BEFORE MORGDRON DISAPPEARED, AND FERGUSON AND MORGDRON WERE ASSOCIATES. THERE'S DEFINITELY A CONNECTION.
EVEN MORE GROTESQUE, WAS THAT MUTILATION MURDER OF GREGORY ASKINS.
HMMM... DELICIOUS! IT'S THE OTHER KIND OF WHITE MEAT,
LONG PIG!
...OH YES! A DELICACY FOR ONLY THE GRATUITOUSLY INDULGENT!
HE'D BEEN STRUNG UP IN HIS APARTMENT BACK AT PERFECTOWN. HIS FLESH HAD BEEN SLICED FROM HIS BODY WITH SHARP KNIVES AND HIS REMAINS WERE COVERED IN VICIOUS BITES. ASKINS, ALSO A FRIEND OF MORGDRON'S, HAD BEEN PARTIALLY EATEN. IT'S OBVIOUS HE WAS THE VICTIM OF PHASE TWO REGENS, WHO LIKE THEIR MEAT RAW AND ALIVE!
TWO WITNESSES PUT GLORIA MCKAI AND RAE DAWSON IN THE VICINITY AT THE TIME...
...NOT FAR AWAY AND DOWNRIVER...
NO ESCAPE FOR YOU THIS TIME, MISSY!
WE GOTCHA NOW!
SHIT! I DON'T BELIEVE THIS!
...IT'S THAT SAME SPASTIC CLAN!
AND I SWEAR, THERE'S EVEN MORE OF THEM, NOW!
HOW ARE WE GOING TO GET OUT OF THIS!?
ONLY ONE WAY I KNOW... THE HARD WAY!

SHIT! BOUNCED STRAIGHT OFF!
P-TWU!
THLUP!
THAT'S NOT GONNA STOP ME, GIRLIE!
K'NEL! DIDN'T EVEN FLINCH!
SLUT!
...CAN'T TAKE 'EM OUT... CRIPPLE 'EM. SLOW 'EM DOWN!
SHIT!
THWP!

HEAR THAT? VIOLENT FUGLY ACTIVITY UP AHEAD...
KBOOM!
CALL IT A HUNCH, BUT THOSE TWO MURDEROUS SLUTS HAVE GOT TO BE INVOLVED, SOMEHOW. WHO ELSE OUT HERE HAS GUNS?
NIAAGH!
THUK!
THEY'VE ONLY GOT PEA SHOOTERS! CAN'T DO ANY LASTIN' DAMAGE ...AND THEY'VE GOT TERRIBLE AIM!
NOW GET IN THERE AND GET THEM, YOU DAFT RETARDS!
...AN' DON'T FERGET!
WE WANT 'EM ALIVE, AND YOU KNOW WHY!
CLAN FIGHTING UP-RIVER!
BUT NOT OUR CLAN.
THEY'RE ON OUR TERRITORY!

...THE TWO CLANS RAPIDLY ENGAGED IN BRUTAL CONFLICT.
MOTHER MAGAERA WAS ENRAGED BY THE MOTHERS MAGDAGALA CLAN'S TRESPASSING INTO HER TERRITORY...
GRRRAAHRG!
GOOD THING THOSE TWO ARE PREOCCUPIED!
THUK!
NOW'S THE PERFECT TIME TO QUIETLY SLIP AWAY...
MINUTES LATER, BOTH CLAN LEADERS WERE LOCKED IN SAVAGE COMBAT AND OBLIVIOUS TO ALL ELSE.
...PRESENTLY....
THIS'S SOME FREAK SHOW! ...BATTLE OF THE FUGLIES!
...KEEP OUT OF SIGHT. WE CAN ILL AFFORD TO BECOME A PART OF THIS ONE.
CAN'T SEE ANY SIGN OF THOSE TWO SKANKY BITCHES,
...THAT GUNFIRE HAD TO HAVE COME FROM THEM...

I SEE THEM! ...SKULKING TOWARDS THAT GULLY!
STAY LOW AND REMAIN WITHIN THAT SAME GULLY, ...SHOULD BE ABLE TO AVOID THE FUGLIES...
...AND TAKE THOSE TWO PHASE TWOS BY SURPRISE!
...ON ENTERING THE GULLY, THERE WAS INSTANT TROUBLE...
FOR FUCK'S SAKE!
IT'S ONLY A STRAY,
I'LL SEE TO THIS, YOU KEEP GOING...
...SOME MINUTES LATER...
YOU'RE GONNA DIE OUT HERE YOU DUMB SLUT!
THERE THEY ARE!
...JUST OVER THERE!
SHIT DREG LITTLE SLAGS MUST'VE SPOTTED ME!
...NOT SURE HOW...
WHERE IS SHE, GLORIA? ...CAN'T SEE ANYTHING!
SHE'S CLOSE, JUST BEHIND THAT ROCK.
I'LL KEEP HER BUSY FROM THIS SIDE WHILE YOU GO GET HER FROM THE OTHER... ...NOW GO!
BLAMM! BLAMM!
KOOM!
END OF THE LINE,
SPASTIC MUTANT WHORE!
KOOM!

THLP!
KU-THOOM!
THAK!
FINALLY DROPPED THE FREAK! TOOK ENOUGH ROUNDS!
AT THE SAME INSTANT...
FHOOMP!
FUMPE! FOOMP!
TIME FOR YOU TO JOIN YOUR WHORE-MAGGOT GIRLFRIEND, SLAG!
...IT'S OVER!
I SEE YOU WASTED NO TIME WASTING THEM...
...SURE YOU PUT ENOUGH ROUNDS IN THEM?
THEY HAD IT COMING...
THEY'RE REGENS, THEY'LL LIVE...
BUT THEY WON'T BE DOING ANYTHING OR GOING ANYWHERE FOR A VERY LONG TIME...

HERE'S THE GRUEL TRUCK.
THAT CRAP AIN'T EVEN MEAT! IT'S SYNTHETIC BILGE PUMPED FULL OF CHEMICALS. NO WONDER WE'RE ALL CONSTANTLY SICK AS SHIT!
WE'RE GONNA ROT IN HERE!
18 MONTHS LATER, IN A STATE OF THE ART, HIGH SECURITY PRISON LOCATED DEEP IN THE SUBTERRANEAN BOWELS OF PERFECTOWN...
WE'LL GET OUT OF HERE...
JUST BE PATIENT. UNLIKE THE REST OF HUMANITY, WE HAVE ETERNITY.
I DON'T WANNA WAIT FOR AN ETERNITY, RAE!
NO WAY I'M EATIN' THAT SLOP TODAY. I'M GETTIN' SOME REAL MEAT. YOU WITH ME, RAE?
I KNOW JUST WHAT YOU MEAN BY THAT, GLORIA.
BUT I'VE GOT TO WARN YOU WE DO IT TOO OFTEN, WE'LL MAKE TOO MANY ENEMIES IN HERE...
FIRST DECENT MEAL I'VE HAD IN WAY TOO LONG.
WE REALLY CAN'T KEEP DOING THIS. SOONER OR LATER...
BULLSHIT, RAE...
WE'RE NOT THE ONLY GIRLS WHO DO THIS. BESIDES, YOU WANNA KEEP UP YOUR COMPLEXION, DON'T YOU?
...WELL, SHUT UP AND KEEP EATING!
FIN

HYBRIDOS
THE LOST PLANET
LONG BEFORE HUMANITY APPEARED UPON THE EARTH, IN A DISTANT PART OF THE GALAXY, THERE WAS A MASSIVE SUPERNOVA EXPLOSION.
BY S. CARTER AND A. RYDYR © 2010
RADIATION FROM THIS AWESOME STELLA EVENT BATHED SEVERAL NEIGHBOURING SOLAR SYSTEMS, ONE OF WHICH HARBOURED AN ISOLATED AND AT ONE TIME EARTHLIKE PLANET NOW KNOWN AS HYBRIDOS.
THE COURSE OF EVOLUTION UPON HYBRIDOS WAS PROFOUNDLY ALTERED. UPON ITS DISCOVERY, THE INTERSTELLAR FEDERATION BRANDED IT A HOSTILE, INHOSPITABLE WORLD.
ANY NOTION OF SENDING A MANNED EXPEDITION THERE WAS VIEWED BY THE AUTHORITIES AS A POINTLESS, UNACCEPTABLY DANGEROUS AND PROHIBITIVELY EXPENSIVE VENTURE.
BUT THAT DIDN'T STOP THOSE WHO WANTED TO SEE HYBRIDOS FOR THEMSELVES.
WHEN OUR ANCESTORS CRASH-LANDED HERE AEONS AGO, THE PROSPECTS OF THEIR SURVIVAL WERE GRIM.
NO RESCUE EFFORT WAS FORTHCOMING; HYBRIDOS IS A FORGOTTEN WORLD.

OVER SEVERAL GENERATIONS WE HAVE PERSISTED. THE TECHNOLOGY WHICH WE BROUGHT WITH US IS LONG GONE, PERISHED WITH TIME. THE HIGH TECHNOLOGICAL WORLD OF OUR ORIGIN IS NOW A DISTANT DREAM, FOREVER LOST.
WE HAVE FORGED WHAT UTENSILS WE NEED FROM THE RESOURCES AVAILABLE TO US ON THIS VIOLENT WORLD AND DO WHAT WE MUST TO SURVIVE.
S. CARTER
2010

LIFE ON THIS PLANET IS A PERPETUAL STATE OF WAR. ALL OF US ARE WARRIORS, MEN, WOMEN, EVEN CHILDREN.
WE FIGHT TO LIVE, TO SURRENDER IS TO DIE. THE LEGACY OF THAT ANCIENT SUPERNOVA HAS PERMEATED ALL INDIGENOUS LIFE HERE—
— A MENAGERIE OF LETHAL HYBRIDS, INTERMINGLING GENES AND FORMS CONSTANTLY PREYING ON ONE ANOTHER,
— YET ALSO INTERBREEDING, CREATING MORE HYBRIDS, EACH ONE A MONSTROSITY, BATTLING, FEEDING, KILLING, EVOLVING — THIS IS HYBRIDOS.
DURING EMPEROR URLU'S REIGN, WE FOUGHT THE HYBRIDOS BROOD QUEENS WHENEVER THEY APPEARED IN OUR DOMAIN, AND SUFFERED HEAVY LOSSES EVERY TIME.
THIS CANNOT BE SUSTAINED WITHOUT EVENTUALLY DESTROYING OURSELVES.
TO CONTINUE THIS COURSE OF ACTION IS TO LOSE THE WAR AND BECOME EXTINCT!
BROOD QUEENS ARE VERY DIFFERENT TO THE MONGREL HORDES WHICH HAVE BEEN ASSAILING US.
THEY ARE A HIGHER EVOLUTION OF HYBRIDOS LIFE...
— INTELLIGENT, CAN BE BARGAINED WITH...
3

INEVITABLY, WE'VE BECOME A PART OF IT. EVER SINCE OUR ANCESTORS WERE STRANDED HERE, HUMAN DNA HAS BEEN INTEGRATED INTO THE SAVAGE, WRITHING GENETIC STREAM OF HYBRIDOS.

THOSE LOYAL TO EMPRESS DASA SOON DISCOVERED OUR INTENTIONS.

EMPRESS, IT'S A MATTER OF UTMOST URGENCY, THE USURPERS, DRAN AND TREN HAVE PUT TOGETHER A BAND OF REBELS! THEY ARE HEADED FOR THE BROOD QUEEN'S DEN AS WE SPEAK!

WRETCHED TRAITORS! THEY'LL RUIN EVERYTHING I'VE ACHIEVED!

THAT BROOD QUEEN AND HER SPAWN ARE ALL THAT STANDS BETWEEN OUR ANNIHILATION FROM THE MINDLESS HYBRIDOS HORDES AND SALVATION! THOSE MUTINEERS MUST BE STOPPED, YULA! GATHER YOUR FORCES, GET AFTER THEM!

YES, EMPRESS DASA.

WE CAME FROM EARTH BUT NOW HYBRIDOS IS OUR HOME. IT IS CLEAR WE CANNOT FIGHT THEM AND WIN. WE CAN NO LONGER REMAIN AS SCATTERED ENCLAVES OF HUMANS AND EXPECT TO SURVIVE AS A SPECIES.

WE HAVE TO ASSIMILATE. LIFE, EVOLUTION AND PROGRESS, TO ADAPT AND SURVIVE. THAT IS WHAT IT HAS ALWAYS BEEN ABOUT, ON EARTH, HERE ON HYBRIDOS, EVERYWHERE. WE MUST DO LIKEWISE OR PERISH!

5

THE HYBRIDOS ARE GRADUALLY CHANGING, ASSIMILATING OUR GENES, EVOLVING. THE TIME WILL COME WHEN WE WILL BECOME ONE WITH THE GREATER HYBRIDOS ECOSPHERE. THIS IS OUR DESTINY, NOW. ALL PRODUCE THAT WE CONSUME IS NATIVE TO THIS PLANET, AND IT IS CHANGING US. THE HYBRIDOS ARE GENETICALLY COMPATIBLE WITH US; WE ARE BECOMING COMPATIBLE WITH THEM!
"THIS BROOD QUEEN IS THE BRIDGE BETWEEN OUR PAST HISTORY AND FUTURE.
"WHAT I DARE NOT DIVULGE TO ANYONE, YET, IS WHAT TRANSPIRED ON THE DAY OF THAT FATEFUL BATTLE, WHEN I BARELY ESCAPED WITH MY LIFE AND MY LOVER, EMPEROR URLU, WAS VIOLATED AND KILLED,
"...AND OF THE PROGENY THAT I NOW CARRY!"

YULA'S FORCES RAPIDLY CAUGHT UP WITH US.
BUT WARRIORS SELDOM SETTLE DISPUTES THROUGH DIPLOMACY, IRRESPECTIVE OF THE CIRCUMSTANCES. IT TOOK MOST OF THE DAY TO REPEL THEM.
ON A PLANET FULL OF PREDATORS THAT REGARD HUMANS AS EASY PREY THE LAST THING WE NEEDED WAS TO BE FIGHTING AMONGST OURSELVES.
AS MANY FIGHTERS WERE TAKEN BY THE CARNIVOROUS PLANTS BELOW AS FROM THE FEROCIOUS BATTLE ITSELF.

THE MOMENT WE ENTERED THE BROOD QUEEN'S DEN, HER SUBORDINATE SISTERS RALLIED TO HER DEFENSE.
EACH ONE OF THEM WOULD, ONE DAY, BECOME A BROOD QUEEN IN HER OWN RIGHT, PROVIDING THEY SURVIVED THE AGGRESSIVE COMPETITION AMONGST THEMSELVES AND THE REST OF THE MULTITUDE OF HYBRIDOS LIFE.
FOR NOW, THEY HAD US TO CONTEND WITH, AND WE ARE VETERANS OF THIS WAR. IT'S THE ONLY LIFE WE KNOW.
MONSTROUS, MALFORMED FEATURES OF WOMEN WERE EVIDENT IN THE STARTLING ANATOMY OF THEM ALL — A GENETIC MELANGE OF INFINITE DIVERSITY, WITH EACH CREATURE BEING TOTALLY UNIQUE.
THEY KEPT COMING; WE KEPT SLAYING THEM...
8

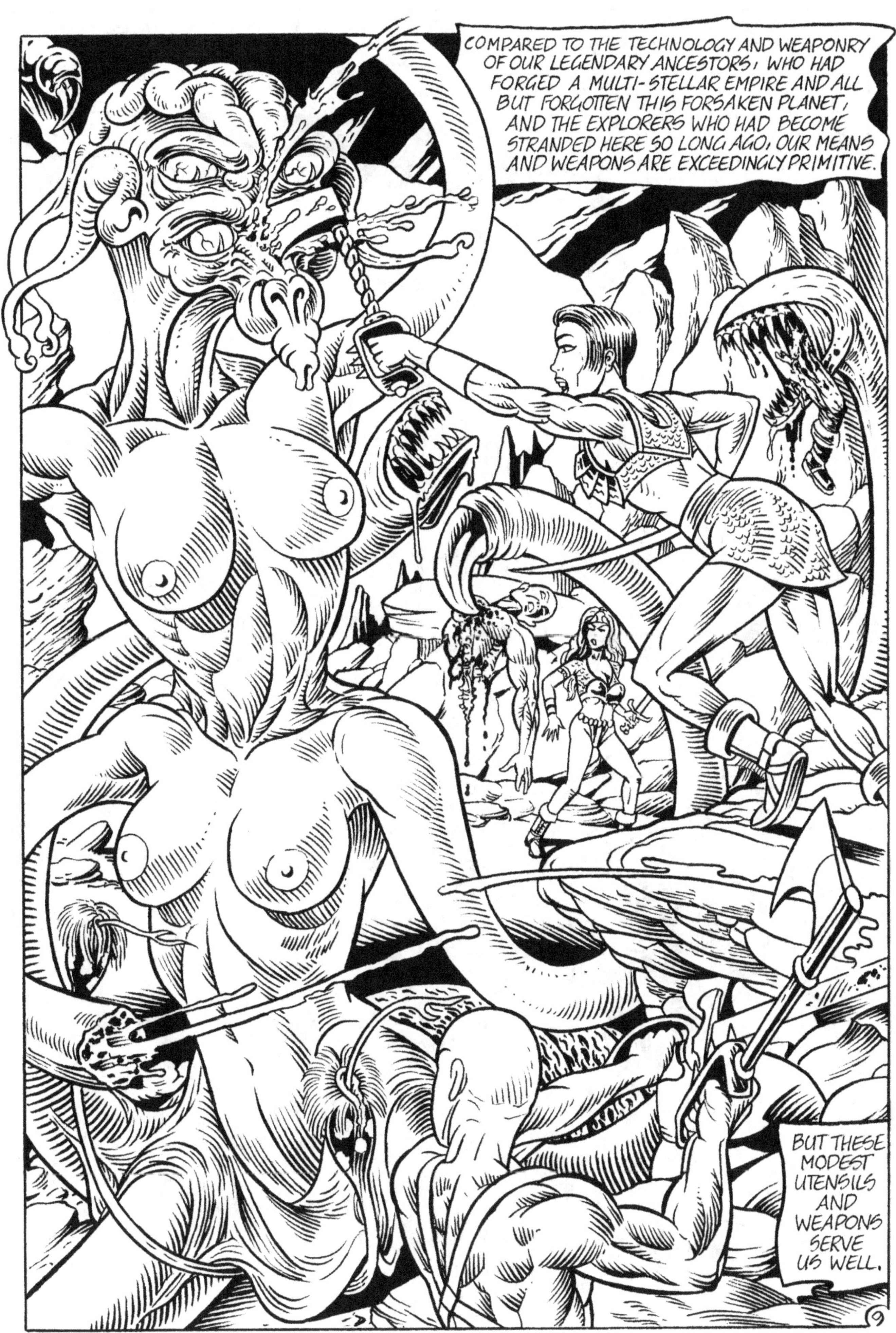

COMPARED TO THE TECHNOLOGY AND WEAPONRY OF OUR LEGENDARY ANCESTORS, WHO HAD FORGED A MULTI-STELLAR EMPIRE AND ALL BUT FORGOTTEN THIS FORSAKEN PLANET, AND THE EXPLORERS WHO HAD BECOME STRANDED HERE SO LONG AGO, OUR MEANS AND WEAPONS ARE EXCEEDINGLY PRIMITIVE.
BUT THESE MODEST UTENSILS AND WEAPONS SERVE US WELL.

I WAS THE ONE WHO FINALLY DELIVERED THE DEATH BLOW TO THAT INFERNAL BROOD QUEEN, BUT I'D HAVE NEVER BEEN ABLE TO IF IT HADN'T BEEN FOR THE SUPPORT AND SACRIFICE OF MANY OF THOSE WITH ME, ESPECIALLY DRAN, WHOSE INHERENT LEADERSHIP SKILLS HAD COME TO THE FORE AND PLAYED A CRUCIAL ROLE IN MAINTAINING UNITY AND DISCIPLINE WITHIN OUR DEDICATED BAND OF WARRIORS. I FELT BLESSED, WHILE SO MANY LIVES HAD BEEN LOST, ALL I HAD LOST DURING THE HEAT OF BATTLE WAS MY SWORD'S SCABBARD, TORN AWAY BY THE HOOKED APPENDAGE OF SOME UNKNOWN BEAST.
ON RETURNING, WE WERE CONFRONTED BY A GRUESOME SPECTACLE WITHIN THE GREAT HALL.
THAT! THAT IS WHAT OUR DERANGED EMPRESS WOULD HAVE US ALL BECOME!
ARE THERE ANY AMONG YOU NOW, WHO ARE TRULY PREPARED TO ACCEPT SUCH A FATE?
FORTUNATELY FOR US AND ALL OF HUMANITY, EMPRESS DASA'S REIGN WAS A SHORT ONE.
A STUNNED, DEATHLIKE SILENCE SUFFICED AS MY ANSWER.
SCAR © 2010
END

UNWORLD - THE WORLD BEFORE THE DELUGE
BATTLE OF THE BRUTES
BY STEVE CARTER AND ANTOINETTE RYDYR © 2007/8
IN THE AEONS BEFORE THE GREAT FLOOD HYBRID RACES AND MONSTROUS BEASTS LIVED UPON THE EARTH ALONGSIDE MANKIND.
IT HAS BEEN SAID THAT A PHANTASMAL VERSION OF THIS VASTLY ARCHAIC EARTH STILL EXISTS AND THAT IT IS EVER UNCHANGING YET ALSO CONSTANTLY EVOLVING
IT IS KNOWN AS THE UNWORLD AND CAN BE FOUND IN A MYSTERIOUS REALM WHERE DREAMS, NIGHTMARES, MYTHOLOGY AND REALITY HAVE BECOME INEXTRICABLY MERGED TOGETHER.

THIS IS NO ORDINARY MEDUSOID! IT'S A GORGON-HYDRA, ONE OF MANY MEDUSOID GODDESSES WORSHIPPED BY THE ACCURSED GORGONEONS.
LOOK, DRUK! NEW HEADS ARE GROWING FROM THE MEDUSOID'S SEVERED NECKS!
HOW ARE WE EVER GOING TO KILL THIS CREATURE?
I'M NOT CERTAIN IT CAN BE KILLED. ITS WOUNDS HEAL THE MOMENT WE INFLICT THEM.
ONLY THE TWO OF US LEFT, AGUL! WE HAVE NO CHANCE AGAINST THAT THING NOW!
...TIME TO RUN!
WE HAVE TO WARN THE VILLAGE!
WHY IS THAT THING HERE, SO FAR FROM IT'S DWELLING PLACE IN THE MANDRAGOR WOOD?
...THE GORGONEONS! ~ THEY SENT IT TO KILL US!
...BUT THEY CAN NO MORE CONTROL THE ACTIONS OF THE MEDUSOIDS ~ OR ANY OTHER DWELLERS OF THE MANDRAGOR WOOD ~ THAN WE!
PERHAPS THEY HAVE FOUND A WAY TO DO SO THROUGH BLACK WITCHERY!

ONCE WE CROSS TO THE OTHER SIDE WE'LL BE SAFE.
MAYBE NOT.
THAT GORGON-HYDRA IS PROBABLY ON ITS WAY TO ATTACK OUR VILLAGE.
AND IT WAS A MERE ACT OF FATE THAT OUR HUNTING PARTY ENCOUNTERED IT FIRST...
RAVENHEARTS! ~ SCOURGE OF THE SKIES!
FORTUNATELY, THEY'RE NOT INTERESTED IN US...
BUT THERE'LL BE MORE OF THEM SOON.
...COMING TO FEAST UPON WHAT'S LEFT OF OUR COMPANIONS!
THEY'LL FIND VERY LITTLE.
THAT MEDUSOID WAS GORGING ITSELF, EVEN AS WE FOUGHT IT.

DRUK, AGUL! WHY ARE YOU BACK SO SOON?
WHERE IS THE REST OF YOUR PARTY?
YOU LOOK EXHAUSTED! WHAT HAS HAPPENED?
WE WERE ATTACKED BY A GIANT MEDUSOID!
THE OTHERS ARE DEAD!
GATHER THE WARRIORS, NOW.
THERE IS PRECIOUS LITTLE TIME!
THEY ARE AFTER THE FAERONS, WARLORD, WHO CONSTANTLY TORMENT THEM AND SNATCH AWAY THEIR MEN!
YES, MEN WHOSE LIVES WE HAVE SAVED FROM BEING SACRIFICED IN THEIR BLOODTHIRSTY FERTILITY RITES.
...MEN THAT THE GORGONEONS ABDUCTED FROM THE VILLAGES OF THE MANLINGS IN THE FIRST PLACE!
THIS ATTACK BY ADRAXIA, QUEEN OF THE GORGONEONS AND HER ARMY WAS INEVITABLE!
NOT ONLY HAVE THOSE BRUTAL AMAZONS ALWAYS BEEN OUR ENEMIES, BUT ALSO, SINCE ERAMIS HERE AND HER FAERON SISTERS HAVE BEEN LIVING HERE UNDER OUR PROTECTION, THE GORGONEONS HAVE INCREASED THEIR ATTACKS UPON US...

4

YOU PROMISED TO PROTECT US FROM THE GORGONEONS, GREAT WARLORD GROKUL. AND AS A DISPLAY OF OUR ETERNAL GRATITUDE, WE HAVE LAVISHED UPON YOU AND ALL TAURIONS, MORE PLEASURES THAN ANY WOMAN OF THE MANLINGS EVER COULD!
WE GIVE YOU FREELY WHAT YOU CAN ONLY OBTAIN FROM ANY MANLING'S WOMAN THROUGH BRUTE FORCE. WE BEAR YOUR SONS, DUTIFULLY PERFORM ALL MANNER OF CHORES AND TASKS,,,
WE DO EVERY-THING FOR YOU!
DO NOT WORRY, MY PRETTY FAERON. YOU WILL ALWAYS BE MY ADORABLE AND DEVOTED WIFE! THE PROTECTION OF THE TAURIONS REMAINS.
WE EXIST FOR NO OTHER REASON THAN TO COMBAT THE SCOURGE OF THE GORGONEONS, WHO WILL FOREVER BE OUR ETERNAL FOES!
NOT FAR AWAY...
THE GORGON HYDRA MADE SHORT WORK OF THAT TAURION HUNTING PACK!
AND I'M CERTAIN, ADRAXIA MY QUEEN, THAT THE GIANT MEDUSOID SHALL EASILY BREACH THE WALLS OF THEIR SMALL VILLAGE.
YES, I AM MOST PLEASED, NABAERA. THIS TIME, WE'LL RAZE THAT TAURION VILLAGE!
...AND KILL EVERY ONE OF THOSE MALICIOUS LITTLE FAERONS WE FIND THERE!
IT'S ESPECIALLY IMPORTANT THAT WE SLAY THEIR QUEEN, ERAMIS.
SHE'S VENOMOUS AND DEADLY!

5

SO, THE GRAND TAURION WARLORD IS TRULY BESOTTED BY THE MALIGNANT FAERON QUEEN! YOU SICKEN ME TO THE BLACK PIT OF MY DARK SOUL, GROKUL!
YOU ARE AS FEEBLE AS THE MANLING DABBLERS IN SORCERY THAT CREATED YOUR BREED SO THAT YOU MIGHT FIGHT THEIR WARS FOR THEM.
AFTER YOU CONQUERED US, WE WERE TO BE YOUR CONCUBINES AND THE MOTHERS OF ALL NEW GENERATIONS OF TAURIONS!
INSTEAD, YOU LUSTED AFTER AND RAVISHED THE LAME-MINDED WOMEN OF THE MANLINGS, WHO ALL LOOK UPON YOU AS GROTESQUE ABERRATIONS OF NATURE!
YOU WERE TOO LAZY TO FIGHT US, TOO DULL-WITTED TO BEFRIEND US!
AS ALLIES, WE MIGHT HAVE SUBJUGATED ALL OF THE MANLING KINGDOMS AND SHARED THE SPOILS.
BUT NOW IT IS YOU WHO HAS BEEN SUBJUGATED! THE SCHEMING FAERONS HAVE MADE YOU AS DOMESTICATED AS THE CATTLE IN YOUR PENS.
ALL TAURIONS ARE FIT ONLY FOR SLAUGHTER!

NO TAURION AXE OR SWORD CAN KILL IT! RELEASE THE ABOMINATION FROM THE PIT!
ARE YOU CERTAIN, DRUK?
WE NEED EVERY TAURION HERE TO REPEL THE GORGONEON FORCES. LET THE ABOMINATION LOOSE ON THAT MEDUSOID, ... NOW!
IT'S FREE! NOW RUN!
THE ABOMINATION DOES NOT DISCRIMINATE.
STAY CLEAR OF IT!

WHAT ARE YOU DOING? STAY UNDER COVER! ONLY DEATH AWAITS YOU IN THE SKY!
IT'S NOT GOOD ENOUGH FOR US TO HIDE IN THE CELLARS AND TREMBLE WHILE THE GORGONEONS SACK OUR NEW HOMES!
OUR BELOVED PROTECTORS NEED US!
VERY NOBLE OF YOU, DARSI, BUT YOU'LL BE OF NO USE IF YOU DIE!
DIE? WE HAVE FOUGHT THE GORGONEONS COUNTLESS TIMES, ERAMIS,
AND WE ALWAYS WIN!
NOT WHEN THE SKY IS FULL OF RAVENHEARTS!
NOW WAIT! LISTEN TO ERAMIS!
KILL EVERY ONE OF THOSE VILE LITTLE WITCHES YOU CAN!

TIME YOU LEARNED, FAERON!

IT IS WE WHO RULE THE SKIES HERE!

YOU ARE A CENTURIES-OLD HARRIDAN LOCKED WITHIN A MANLING'S WHORE, ADRAXIA! IT IS I WHO SHALL FREE YOUR TAINTED SPIRIT FROM ITS PRISON OF FLESH!

...WITH ONE BLOW OF MY SWORD!

YOU HAVE BECOME A WEAKLING, GROKUL! THE FAERONS HAVE MADE YOU TOO COMPLACENT,

DRAINED YOU OF YOUR STRENGTH,

AND WILL TO FIGHT!

THEIR SEDUCTIONS ARE THEIR WEAPONS!

...SPELLS THAT MAKE YOU TORPID AS THEY SAP YOUR VIGOUR

YOU ARE NO LONGER A WILD TAURION BULL!

...MERELY A CALF TO BE BUTCHERED!

MEANWHILE...

NOT EVEN THE MIGHT OF THE ABOMINATION CAN STOP THAT ACCURSED MEDUSOID!

PERHAPS I CAN

HOW, ERAMIS? WHAT CAN A FAERON DO THAT THE MOST SKILLED WARRIORS AND POWERFUL OF BEASTS CANNOT?

I AM NOT JUST ANY FAERON, DRUK,

I'M THEIR QUEEN!

ERAMIS WAS SWIFT, HER AIM TRUE,
ADRAXIA, MY QUEEN, YOU HAVE BEEN WOUNDED!
THE MEDUSOID! THAT IMPISH FAERON QUEEN HAS SLAIN IT!
THE TIP OF ERAMIS' PIKE WAS DIPPED IN HER VENOM! SHE DROVE IT INTO ITS HEART! IT FELT AS IF MY HEART HAD BEEN PIERCED!

LET ME HELP YOU.
WHILE THE MEDUSOID LIVED, I WAS ABLE TO COMMAND IT,
THAT IS TRUE, AND NOW, WE HAVE THE ABOMINATION TO CONTEND WITH!
I WILL BE FINE IN A MOMENT
BUT THE ADVANTAGE WE HAD HAS NOW BEEN LOST!
ERAMIS' VENOM BROKE THE SPELL BUT YOUR SORCERY HAS DONE ITS WORK.
MEANWHILE,
YOU KILLED IT WITH A SINGLE STRIKE!
YET, WHEN ONE OF OUR SPEARS STRUCK THAT VERY SAME SPOT IT HAD NO EFFECT!
EXCEPT FOR THOSE RAVENHEARTS, NOTHING FEMALE IS IMMUNE TO MY VENOM.
THAT INCLUDES ALL THE MEDUSOIDS!
WHEN ONE OF US BECOMES A QUEEN HER SALIVA CHANGES,
AND THERE CAN BE ONLY ONE QUEEN IN ANY SINGLE COMMUNITY OF FAERONS AT A TIME,
YOU HAVE NOTHING TO FEAR, DRUK. MY VENOM DOES NOT HARM MALES.

ONCE THE MEDUSOID HAD BEEN SLAIN, THE GORGONEONS WERE FORCED TO RETREAT FROM THE UNSTOPPABLE ONSLAUGHT OF THE ABOMINATION.
LEGENDS TELL THAT THE MONSTROSITY PURSUED THE GORGONEONS AS FAR AS THE MANDRAGOR WOOD WHERE IT MANAGED TO ALL BUT DECIMATE THEIR FORCES BEFORE THEY FINALLY KILLED IT.

THE BATTLE WAS OVER BUT THE DANGER HAD NOT ABATED.
STAY UNDER COVER. ONCE THEY FINISH GORGING, THEY WILL LEAVE.
15

MANLING SORCERERS CREATED US TO FIGHT THE GORGONEONS. WE HAVE BATTLED THEM COUNTLESS TIMES, YET I STILL KNOW SO LITTLE ABOUT THEM.
ARE THEY A RENEGADE ARMY OF MORTAL WOMEN, A REBELLIOUS BAND OF AMAZONS FROM HELLENICIA? I'VE HEARD SO MANY DIFFERENT STORIES...
NO ONE REALLY KNOWS. LEGENDS TELL OF A MURDEROUS RACE OF AMAZONS WHO ARE THE PROGENY OF THE UNION OF MANLINGS AND THE MEDUSOIDS...
WHOEVER, WHATEVER THEY ARE, THEY ARE TRULY MAD!
GROKUL FOUGHT BRAVELY, HE MANAGED TO SLAY TWO-SCORE OF THOSE BERSERK GORGONEONS BEFORE ADRAXIA WAS ABLE TO TAKE HIM DOWN!
SHE'D HAVE NEVER BEEN CAPABLE OF SUCH A FEAT HAD HE NOT BEEN SO BATTLE-WEARY!
TRUE AGUL.
IT'S A SHAME SHE STILL LIVES.
ONLY THE MOST HEROIC TAURIONS ARE LAID TO REST HERE. GROKUL IS ONE OF THEM.
YOU ARE THE WARLORD NOW, DRUK.
I MUST SAY, DRUK, YOU HAVE EARNED THAT TITLE WELL,
AND I CAN THINK OF NO MORE SUITABLE WIFE FOR A WARLORD THAN SHE WHO SLEW THE GIANT MEDUSOID!
FIN...

WAR OF THE WINGED WARRIOR WOMEN

"THIS SWARM IS MASSIVE! THEY'RE KNOCKING US OUT OF THE AIR AS IF THEY'RE SWATTING FLIES!"

"NEED IMMEDIATE AIR-SUPPORT, NOW!"

OUR EFFORTS TO ESTABLISH COLONIES ON THE REMOTE PLANET VALKYREI HAVE BEEN PROBLEMATIC AT BEST.

THE PLANET'S ONLY SENTIENT SPECIES, THE DRUGYLLA, ARE WARLIKE. THEIR CLANS ARE IN PERPETUAL CONFLICT WITH ONE ANOTHER.

BY S. CARTER AND A. RYDYR COPYRIGHT © 2011 SKAZ

THE CLAN WE HAD INITIALLY CONTACTED AND PAINSTAKINGLY BUILT UP RELATIONS WITH HAD EVENTUALLY PERMITTED US TO SET UP AN AMBITOUS NEW SETTLEMENT ALONG THE SOUTHERN BORDER OF THEIR TERRITORY.

WITHIN FOUR VALKYREIAN YEARS THEY HAD BEEN DRIVEN OFF BY A LARGER AND FAR MORE AGGRESSIVE CLAN, WHICH IMMEDIATELY DECLARED WAR ON US.

OUR SITUATION HAS BEEN STEADILY DETERIORATING SINCE,
MY YOUNGER BROTHER, SQUADRON LEADER BRUCE GANNON, WAS SLAIN BY DRUGYLLA DURING ONE OF THEIR RELENTLESS ASSAULTS UPON THE COLONY.
FORCED TO ABORT!
NEED IMMEDIATE COVER FIRE!
DESPITE THESE TERRIBLE SETBACKS, WE WERE HERE TO STAY. VALKYREI IS OUR HOME NOW. EARTH IS THIRTY THOUSAND LIGHT YEARS AWAY. THERE IS NO GOING BACK.
BUT THIS COLONY WAS DOOMED IF THESE ONSLAUGHTS CONTINUED UNABATED. OUR SITUATION WAS GRIM. IN THE WILD HOPE THAT WE MIGHT ACTUALLY ACHIEVE SOMETHING, I VOLUNTEERED TO BE PART OF A BIZARRE EXPERIMENT RUN BY THE MYSTERIOUS DOCTOR ROBERTA GREY...
IF THIS GOES TO PLAN, WE'LL BE ABLE TO TURN THE TIDE OF THIS INFERNAL WAR, AGENT GANNON.
IT WILL PAVE THE WAY FOR MYRIAD POSSIBILITIES!
MURDERS TO BE SOLVED,
POLITICAL SECRETS REVEALED!
AS YOU ARE AWARE, AGENT MACK GANNON, THIS IS HIGHLY CLASSIFIED. YOUR CONSCIOUSNESS WILL BE INSTANTLY TRANSFERRED INTO ANOTHER SENTIENT BEING — IN THIS CASE, THE SUBJECT WILL BE AN INDIVIDUAL DRUGYLLA!
YOU WILL KNOW HER EVERY THOUGHT, FEEL EACH EMOTION SHE FEELS. BUT YOU WILL NOT BE ABLE TO CONTROL HER THOUGHTS AND ACTIONS; NOR COMMUNICATE WITH HER, OR US, ONLY OBSERVE AND EXPERIENCE EVERYTHING SHE EXPERIENCES.
YOU WILL EFFECTIVELY BE A PASSENGER, TRAVELLING WITH HER INSIDE HER MIND. YOU WILL BE THE FIRST EARTHMAN TO LEARN THE INTIMATE NATURE OF THE DRUGYLLA, KNOW WHAT IT IS LIKE TO ACTUALLY BE ONE OF THEM!
YOU WILL BECOME THE ULTIMATE SPY!

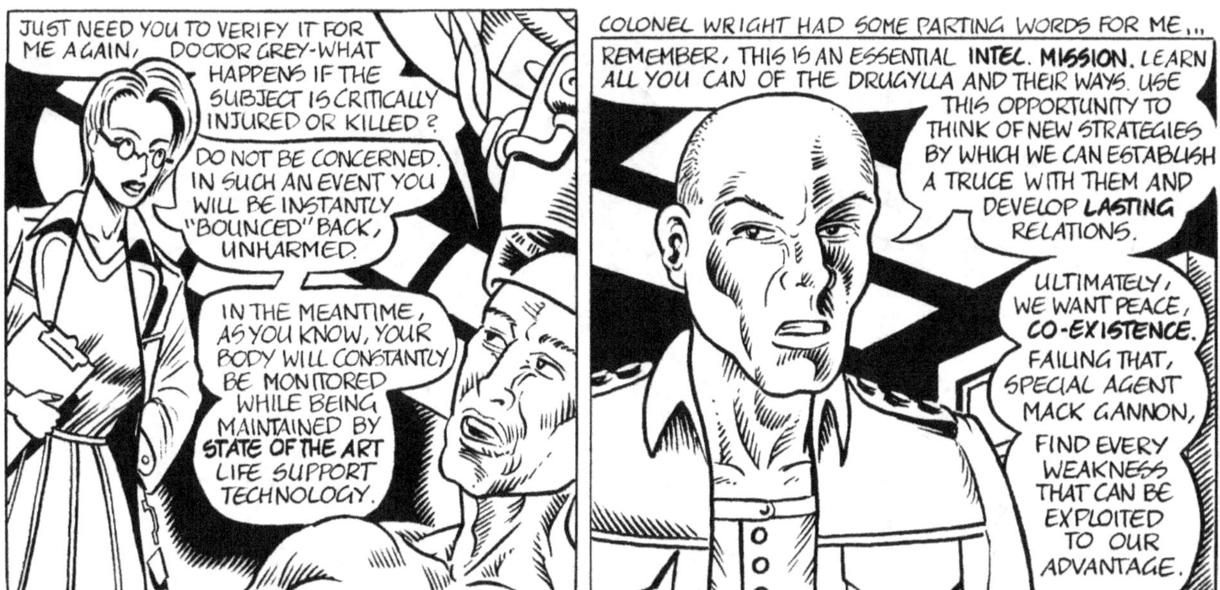

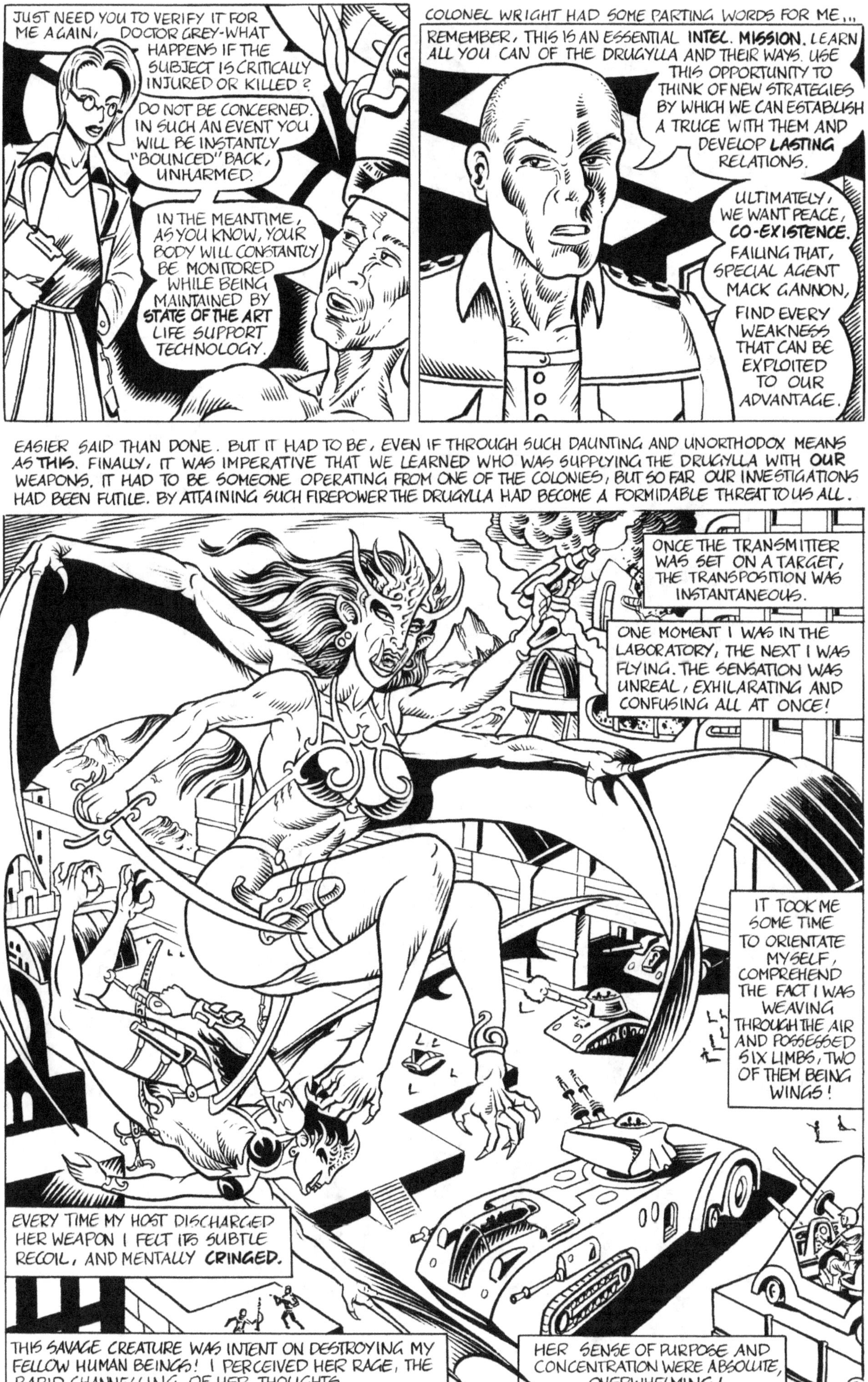

EASIER SAID THAN DONE. BUT IT HAD TO BE, EVEN IF THROUGH SUCH DAUNTING AND UNORTHODOX MEANS AS THIS. FINALLY, IT WAS IMPERATIVE THAT WE LEARNED WHO WAS SUPPLYING THE DRUGYLLA WITH OUR WEAPONS. IT HAD TO BE SOMEONE OPERATING FROM ONE OF THE COLONIES, BUT SO FAR OUR INVESTIGATIONS HAD BEEN FUTILE. BY ATTAINING SUCH FIREPOWER THE DRUGYLLA HAD BECOME A FORMIDABLE THREAT TO US ALL.

ONCE THE TRANSMITTER WAS SET ON A TARGET, THE TRANSPOSITION WAS INSTANTANEOUS.

ONE MOMENT I WAS IN THE LABORATORY, THE NEXT I WAS FLYING. THE SENSATION WAS UNREAL, EXHILARATING AND CONFUSING ALL AT ONCE!

IT TOOK ME SOME TIME TO ORIENTATE MYSELF, COMPREHEND THE FACT I WAS WEAVING THROUGH THE AIR AND POSSESSED SIX LIMBS, TWO OF THEM BEING WINGS!

EVERY TIME MY HOST DISCHARGED HER WEAPON I FELT ITS SUBTLE RECOIL, AND MENTALLY CRINGED.

THIS SAVAGE CREATURE WAS INTENT ON DESTROYING MY FELLOW HUMAN BEINGS! I PERCEIVED HER RAGE, THE RAPID CHANNELLING OF HER THOUGHTS.

HER SENSE OF PURPOSE AND CONCENTRATION WERE ABSOLUTE, OVERWHELMING!

WHAT HAPPENED NEXT WAS HORRIFIC. THERE WAS NOTHING I COULD DO.
SHE MERCILESSLY ATTACKED A GROUP OF UNARMED WORKERS.
USING THE CREST UPON HER HEAD, SHE CLEAVED A MAN'S SKULL NEAR IN TWO. THE IMPACT OF THE BLOW STUNNED ME.
IT WAS A CALCULATED, YET ALSO INTUITIVE, INSTINCTUAL ATTACK.
THE PRIMAL ENERGY THAT SURGED THROUGH HER AS SHE WILDLY ASSAILED HER PREY ENVELOPED ME. I TRIED TO SHUT IT OUT BUT BECAME INEXORABLY TRAPPED IN A MAELSTROM OF HER PRIMITIVE URGES. WHEN IT WAS OVER, SHE TORE OUT THEIR HEARTS AND ATE THEM!
THE TASTE OF HUMAN BLOOD, THE REEK OF BUTCHERED FLESH! — IT WAS TOO MUCH FOR MY ADDLED SENSES!
MY MIND WAS STILL SPINNING LONG AFTER WE'D LEFT THE COLONY AND THE SCENE OF BATTLE FAR BEHIND.
I BECAME ACUTELY AWARE OF THE PHYSICAL POWER OF THIS CREATURE, FELT THE FORCE OF THE WIND AGAINST HER STRENUOUSLY BEATING WINGS.
IT WAS AS THOUGH SHE AND I HAD PHYSICALLY BECOME ONE. THE SHEER ELATION OF FLYING AT SUCH GIDDYING ALTITUDES WAS ECSTATIC!
4

I WAS INTIMATELY LINKED TO HER MIND YET MY THOUGHTS REMAINED INDEPENDENT OF HERS. HER FEELINGS TOWARDS US WERE PAINFULLY EVIDENT. SHE RESENTED OUR PRESENCE, ALONG WITH THE TOLERATION OF US THAT THE VANQUISHED CLAN HAD DISPLAYED.

I WONDERED IF THERE WAS A CHANCE SHE WOULD SOMEHOW DETECT MY PRESENCE, DESPITE DOCTOR GREY'S ASSURANCES THAT SUCH WAS NOT POSSIBLE

VAGUE THOUGHTS I KNEW WERE NOT MINE SWAM IN MY MIND. I DETECTED AN INNATE FASCINATION OF MY KIND THAT MY HOST SECRETLY HARBOURED.

I REALISED HER HATRED HAD BEEN FOSTERED LARGELY THROUGH BONDING WITH HER PEERS AND DEVOTION TO THE CAUSE OF HER CLAN'S LEADERS.

WHILE I FOUND THIS UNSETTLING I DARED NOT DWELL ON IT. THERE WAS IMPORTANT INFORMATION I NEEDED TO ACQUIRE AND PRIORITISE.

MY HOST HAD A NAME — QOGA. SHE WAS WELL RESPECTED WITHIN HER CLAN. LIKE ME, SHE WAS ALSO AN INFILTRATOR SEEKING VITAL INFORMATION — DRUGYLLA DISSIDENTS PLANNED TO ASSASSINATE THE CLAN'S **WAR MISTRESS** AND END THE WAR. QOGA SOUGHT TO IDENTIFY AND DISPATCH THEM.

AS QOGA APPROACHED THE UNARMED AIRMAN I GREW APPREHENSIVE.

I DECIDED THAT I ALSO NEEDED TO LEARN THEIR IDENTITIES...

TERRIFYING, ANCESTRAL PREDATORY URGES SUDDENLY EMERGED FROM SOME DEEP, PRIMORDIAL RECESS OF HER MIND.

EVIDENTLY, THE DRUGYLLA ACCESSED THIS INHERENT FEROCIOUSNESS, WHICH THEY CHANNELLED INTO THEIR RITUALISED RELIGIOUS PRACTICES AND BATTLE-LORE.

AGAIN, I TASTED HUMAN BLOOD AND FLESH! QOGA RELISHED HER CARNAL FEAST, BECAME HIGHLY AROUSED BY HER VICTIM'S ABJECT FEAR. THIS WAS AN ACT OF WANTON BRUTALITY!

IT IGNITED THEIR **WARRIOR PASSION**. RIVALS WERE EATEN ALIVE IN MACABRE CELEBRATORY RITUALS AND THE HEARTS OF SLAIN ENEMIES WERE DEVOURED.

ALL I COULD DO WAS DESPERATELY CLING TO THE HOPE THAT I MIGHT YET UNCOVER EVEN THE VAGUEST TRACE OF HUMANITY LYING SOMEWHERE WITHIN THE DARK ESSENCE OF THIS SAVAGE ALIEN SPECIES. (5)

THROUGH THIS MISSION AND EXPERIMENT WE HAD DELVED INTO COMPLETELY UNKNOWN TERRITORY. HERE, LAY MYSTERIES OF INNER SPACE AND EXISTENCE THAT MIGHT HAVE NEVER BEEN REVEALED, EVEN THROUGH THE FARTHEST EXPLORATION OF DEEP SPACE.
TIJU, WHY DID YOU NOT PARTICIPATE IN THIS SACRED RITUAL OF WAR AND KINSHIP?
THERE IS NOTHING SACRED ABOUT CRUELTY OR TERRORISING THE UNARMED! THE ENEMY MUST BE SLAIN CLEANLY, IN BATTLE, AND ONLY THE HEART OF A WORTHY FOE CAN BE EATEN.
I AM A DRUGYLLA AND A WARRIOR! – NOT A MINDLESS BEAST!
IT WAS CLEAR THAT QOGA SUSPECTED TIJU WAS A PLOTTING DISSIDENT. IF SO, IT WAS WITH TIJU AND HER FELLOW REBELS THAT HOPE FOR CHANGE LAY.
WITHIN SECONDS OF TIJU'S REMARKS, THE PAIR WERE FERVENTLY DUELLING IN THE AIR.
WHEN QOGA SPOKE I UNDERSTOOD HER, JUST AS I WAS ABLE TO INTERPRET HER EMOTIONS AND THOUGHTS. MY MIND WAS LINKED TO HERS AND THE LANGUAGE BARRIER HAD BECOME IRRELEVANT.
HESITANT TO TAKE ON BOTH, TIJU TACTFULLY RETREATED, FLEEING INTO THE DEEP SHADOWS OF A VAST CANYON.
WE'LL NEVER FIND HER NOW, NOT DOWN THERE!
SHE'LL BE BACK, AND WE WILL BE WAITING FOR HER...
OUT OF A LONG HELD RESPECT FOR ALL DRUGYLLA – DESPITE THEIR UNBRIDLED FURY – THEY DID NOT USE THEIR BEAM-GUNS, PREFERRING "TRADITIONAL" BLADES.
FRANTIC MOMENTS LATER, AVEX, THE REMAINING DRUGYLLA, JOINED THE FRAY, SIDING WITH QOGA.
I DID NOT KNOW IF TIJU WAS A REBEL OR NOT, NOR IF SHE WAS SYMPATHETIC TOWARDS THE COLONY. BUT SHE AND QOGA WERE RIVALS. I NOW KNEW THERE WERE DISSIDENTS AMONG THE DRUGYLLA – THIS WAS WITHOUT DOUBT, VITAL INFORMATION.
6

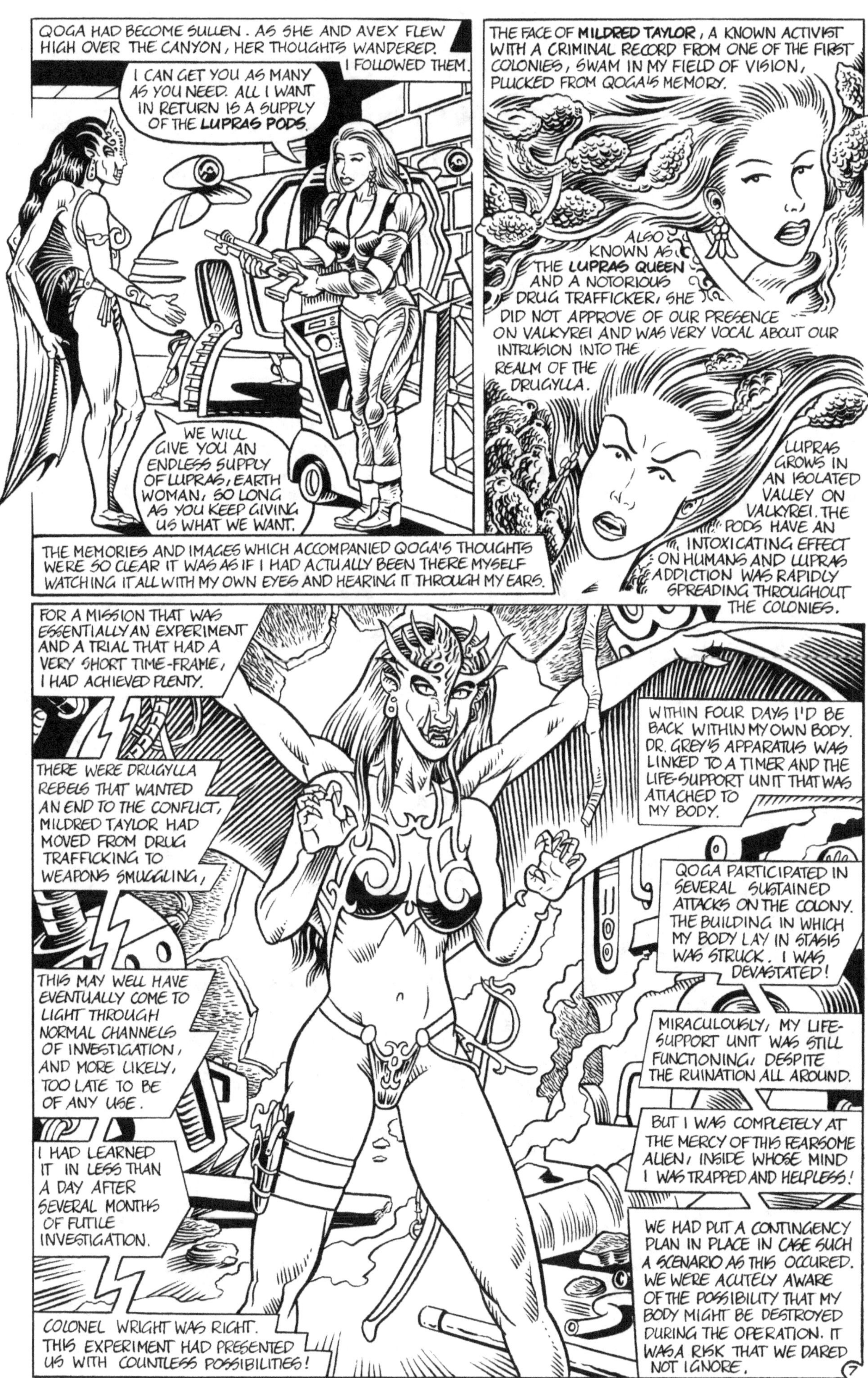

QOGA HAD BECOME SULLEN. AS SHE AND AVEX FLEW HIGH OVER THE CANYON, HER THOUGHTS WANDERED.
I FOLLOWED THEM.
I CAN GET YOU AS MANY AS YOU NEED. ALL I WANT IN RETURN IS A SUPPLY OF THE LUPRAS PODS.
WE WILL GIVE YOU AN ENDLESS SUPPLY OF LUPRAS, EARTH WOMAN, SO LONG AS YOU KEEP GIVING US WHAT WE WANT.
THE MEMORIES AND IMAGES WHICH ACCOMPANIED QOGA'S THOUGHTS WERE SO CLEAR IT WAS AS IF I HAD ACTUALLY BEEN THERE MYSELF WATCHING IT ALL WITH MY OWN EYES AND HEARING IT THROUGH MY EARS.
THE FACE OF MILDRED TAYLOR, A KNOWN ACTIVIST WITH A CRIMINAL RECORD FROM ONE OF THE FIRST COLONIES, SWAM IN MY FIELD OF VISION, PLUCKED FROM QOGA'S MEMORY.
ALSO KNOWN AS THE LUPRAS QUEEN AND A NOTORIOUS DRUG TRAFFICKER, SHE DID NOT APPROVE OF OUR PRESENCE ON VALKYREI AND WAS VERY VOCAL ABOUT OUR INTRUSION INTO THE REALM OF THE DRUGYLLA.
LUPRAS GROWS IN AN ISOLATED VALLEY ON VALKYREI. THE PODS HAVE AN INTOXICATING EFFECT ON HUMANS AND LUPRAS ADDICTION WAS RAPIDLY SPREADING THROUGHOUT THE COLONIES.
FOR A MISSION THAT WAS ESSENTIALLY AN EXPERIMENT AND A TRIAL THAT HAD A VERY SHORT TIME-FRAME, I HAD ACHIEVED PLENTY.
THERE WERE DRUGYLLA REBELS THAT WANTED AN END TO THE CONFLICT, MILDRED TAYLOR HAD MOVED FROM DRUG TRAFFICKING TO WEAPONS SMUGGLING.
THIS MAY WELL HAVE EVENTUALLY COME TO LIGHT THROUGH NORMAL CHANNELS OF INVESTIGATION, AND MORE LIKELY, TOO LATE TO BE OF ANY USE.
I HAD LEARNED IT IN LESS THAN A DAY AFTER SEVERAL MONTHS OF FUTILE INVESTIGATION.
COLONEL WRIGHT WAS RIGHT. THIS EXPERIMENT HAD PRESENTED US WITH COUNTLESS POSSIBILITIES!
WITHIN FOUR DAYS I'D BE BACK WITHIN MY OWN BODY. DR. GREY'S APPARATUS WAS LINKED TO A TIMER AND THE LIFE-SUPPORT UNIT THAT WAS ATTACHED TO MY BODY.
QOGA PARTICIPATED IN SEVERAL SUSTAINED ATTACKS ON THE COLONY. THE BUILDING IN WHICH MY BODY LAY IN STASIS WAS STRUCK. I WAS DEVASTATED!
MIRACULOUSLY, MY LIFE-SUPPORT UNIT WAS STILL FUNCTIONING, DESPITE THE RUINATION ALL AROUND.
BUT I WAS COMPLETELY AT THE MERCY OF THIS FEARSOME ALIEN, INSIDE WHOSE MIND I WAS TRAPPED AND HELPLESS!
WE HAD PUT A CONTINGENCY PLAN IN PLACE IN CASE SUCH A SCENARIO AS THIS OCCURED. WE WERE ACUTELY AWARE OF THE POSSIBILITY THAT MY BODY MIGHT BE DESTROYED DURING THE OPERATION. IT WAS A RISK THAT WE DARED NOT IGNORE.

DOCTOR GREY HAD INSTALLED A DEFAULT SETTING INTO THE SYSTEM. MY MIND — MY ESSENCE — WOULD REMAIN WITHIN THE HOST IN THE EVENT THAT MY BODY WAS LOST. IN EFFECT, I'D REMAIN ALIVE, YET BECOME A "GHOST", AS SHE CALLED IT.
TO FEEL, TASTE AND SMELL YOUR OWN FLESH AND BLOOD AS IT IS BEING CONSUMED.
QOGA HAD NO IDEA IT WAS ME OR THAT I EVEN EXISTED!
I KNEW WHAT QOGA'S INTENTIONS WERE. I CAN ONLY DESCRIBE THEM AS BEING SO MONSTROUS THAT MERE WORDS CANNOT CONVEY THE ABSOLUTE HORROR OF IT. TO WITNESS YOUR OWN MURDER — EXPERIENCE IT FROM THE KILLER'S PERSPECTIVE!
ALL THAT I HAD LEARNED THROUGH THIS WEIRD EXPERIMENT MIGHT NEVER BE DIVULGED, ONLY WHEN MY BANEFUL HOST DIED WOULD I FINALLY BE FREE!
TIJU SUDDENLY APPEARED AS IF OUT OF NOWHERE!
FOR SEVERAL MINUTES THE PAIR OF DRUGYLLA VICIOUSLY FOUGHT AMIDST THE SHAMBLES OF THE LAB.
QOGA SUSTAINED A SERIOUS WOUND — THE LANCING PAIN BURNED LIKE FIRE!
I WOKE UP TO SEE DOCTOR ROBERTA GREY BARKING INTO HER HANDSET. TIJU HAD VANISHED.
GET THE MED-TEAM!
IF NOTHING ELSE, QOGA, YOU WERE A WORTHY OPPONENT!
WORTHY OF BEING DISPOSED OF!
AGENT GANNON IS BACK WITH US!
I FULLY EXPERIENCED QOGA'S DEATH TRAUMA. IT THREW ME INTO A PAROXSYM OF AGONY, THEN I BLACKED OUT —
I REALISED IT WAS OVER; I HAD SURVIVED! MISSION ACCOMPLISHED.
FIN

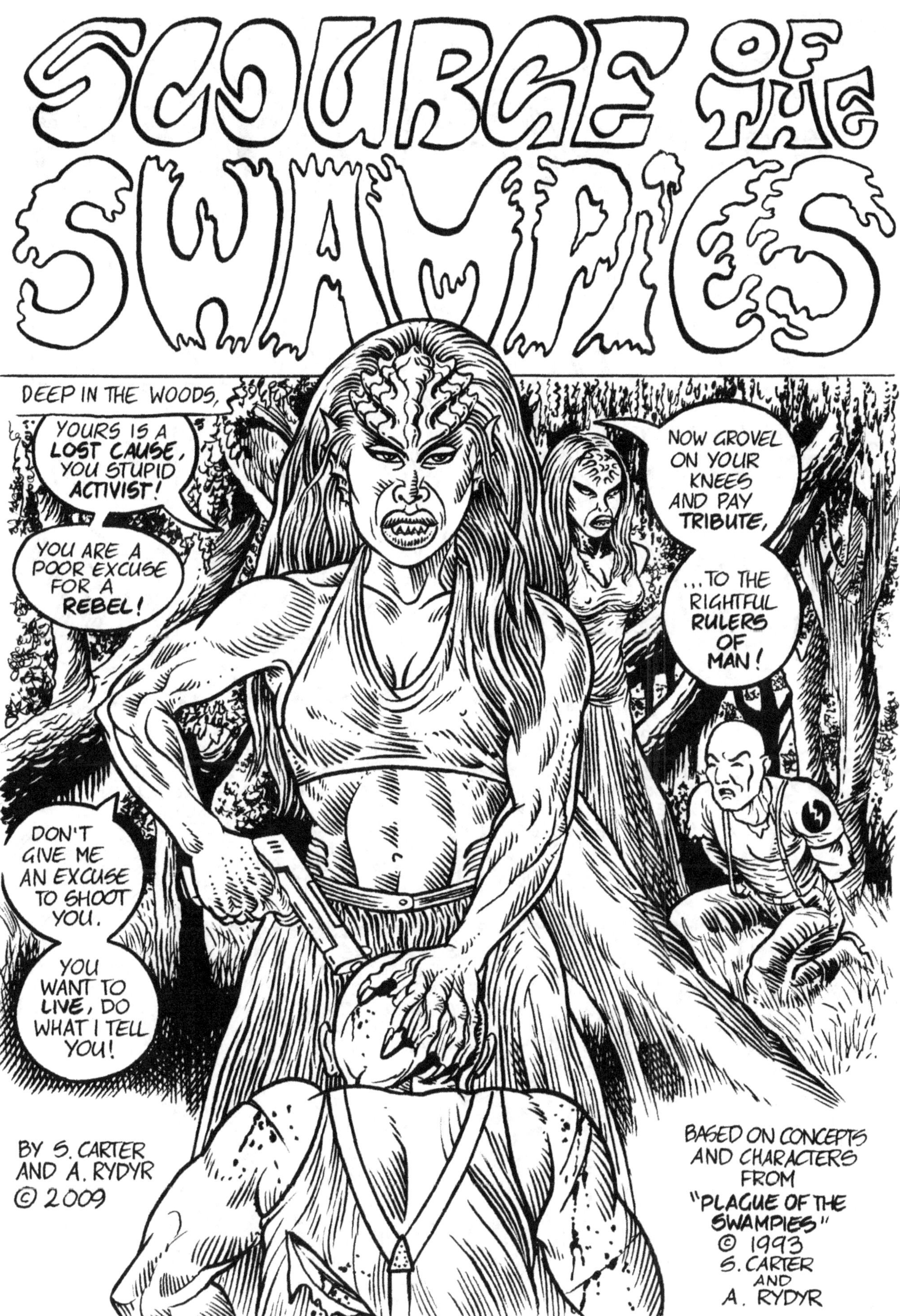

SCOURGE OF THE SWAMPIES

DEEP IN THE WOODS,

YOURS IS A LOST CAUSE, YOU STUPID ACTIVIST!

YOU ARE A POOR EXCUSE FOR A REBEL!

DON'T GIVE ME AN EXCUSE TO SHOOT YOU.

YOU WANT TO LIVE, DO WHAT I TELL YOU!

NOW GROVEL ON YOUR KNEES AND PAY TRIBUTE,

...TO THE RIGHTFUL RULERS OF MAN!

BY S. CARTER AND A. RYDYR © 2009

BASED ON CONCEPTS AND CHARACTERS FROM "PLAGUE OF THE SWAMPIES" © 1993 S. CARTER AND A. RYDYR

WHAT WE NEED, MY SUJUL SISTERS, IS NUMBERS, OR THE SAPIENS WILL ALWAYS BE ONE UP ON US. WE HAVE TO PROCURE MORE MEN!
AND NOW, IN THE STUDIO WITH ME IS THE LEADER OF THE OPPOSITION, MISTER WAYNE HEATH.
YOUR PARTY IS ADVOCATING A POLICY OF SEGREGATION...
C'RECT!
THE EXPERIMENT OF CO-EXISTENCE BETWEEN WE HUMANS AND THE SUJUL — AS THEY REFER TO THEMSELVES, OR SYRENS RUSULKA AND "SWAMPIES" AS THEY ARE KNOWN BY MANY IN THE BROADER COMMUNITY —
HAS FAILED!
THE POLICIES BASED ON APPEASEMENT, IMPLEMENTED BY THE APOLOGISTS OF THE RHETORICAL LEFT, HAVE EXPOSED EVERY MAN, WOMAN AND CHILD IN SOCIETY TO GREAT DANGER! THE GENERAL POPULACE HAS HAD ENOUGH OF THE CHAOS IN OUR CITIES, SUBURBS AND STREETS! THINGS HAVE TO CHANGE!
YES, OF COURSE THERE ARE PROBLEMS WITH THE INTEGRATION OF HUMANS AND SYRENS, AND MORE MUST BE ACHIEVED REGARDING ISSUES OF PUBLIC SAFETY AND AWARENESS,
I RESPECT ANY HUMANITARIAN CAUSE, BUT THE SYRENS ARE NOT HUMAN. THEY ARE VIOLENT FLESH-EATERS AND HYPER-PREDATORY SEXUAL PARASITES.
WE HAVE MONSTERS LIVING IN OUR MIDST!
BUT HIGH-PROFILE CIVIL LIBERTARIANS AND HUMANITARIAN GROUPS ARE COMPARING YOUR PARTY'S SOLUTION TO THE INFAMOUS DETENTION CAMPS OF THE PAST!
2

YOU'RE OVER-SIMPLIFYING THINGS, DON'T YOU THINK? THE SYRENS POSSESS A HUMANLIKE INTELLIGENCE, A HIGHLY DEVELOPED SOCIAL ORDER, AND HAVE BEEN OFFICIALLY RECOGNISED AS A SENTIENT SPECIES THAT IS PROTECTED BY THE SAME LAWS TO WHICH WE ARE BOUND WITHIN SOCIETY—
YES! LAWS WHICH THEY CONSTANTLY BREAK! ASSAULT, ABDUCTION, RAPE, MURDER! DO NOT FORGET — THE SYRENS ARE ALSO PRIMAL BEINGS, MOTIVATED BY INSTINCT, INCAPABLE OF ANY EMPATHY TOWARDS THEIR PREY!
...AND THEIR PREY IS US! MEN LIKE YOU AND I! THEY DEPEND ON US IN ORDER TO REPRODUCE! EACH TIME ONE OF THEM COMES INTO EXISTENCE A MAN DIES! THEY CONVERT US INTO THEM THROUGH SEX! ULTIMATELY, CO-EXISTENCE MEANS THAT MEN WILL DIE! THAT IS UNACCEPTABLE!
LEFTIST APOLOGISTS — THE ENEMY WITHIN!
ERADICATE THE SWAMPY PESTILENCE!
LEFTY SWAMPY PUMPERS, MAN-EATING SEA HAGS! —THE UNHOLY UNION!
AS IT IS, THE GLOBAL POPULATION OF MALES HAS PLUMMETED OVER THE PAST DECADE!
THE SYRENS ARE NOT OUR FRIENDS! THEY ARE A SCOURGE UPON THE HUMAN RACE!
MEANWHILE, OUT ON THE STREETS,

GET YOUR SHOCK BATTONS READY! HERE THEY COME
I DON'T LIKE THOSE STINKIN' SWAMPIES ANY MORE THAN THEY DO, BUT THESE AGITATORS ARE BEING COUNTER-PRODUCTIVE. ALL THEY'RE GONNA ACHIEVE IS MORE CASUALTIES ON THE STREET AND FURTHER CIVIL UNREST!
EXACTLY WHO ARE THEY, ANYWAY?
EVIDENTLY THEY'RE SOME KIND OF MASCULINIST SURVIVALIST RESISTANCE GROUP,
FORMED FROM THE REMNANCE OF A SKINHEAD CULT TO MAKE A UNITED STAND AGAINST THE SYRENS AND FOR MEN'S RIGHTS!
GH' ODD! IT BEGGARS BELIEF!
BELIEVE IT! WORD IS, THEY'RE GAINING SUPPORT! DROVES OF DESPERATE MEN — AND WOMEN — ARE JOINING THEIR RANKS EVERY DAY!
THERE ARE NEW CELLS POPPING UP IN IN EVERY CITY IN THE COUNTRY — THEY'RE BECOMING A THREAT TO SOCIAL STABILITY.
SLAG!
PRICK!

THE RIOT RAPIDLY INTENSIFIED,
MUSCLE-FAGS WITH SHRUNKEN DICKS HYPED UP ON 'ROID-RAGE!
NO WONDER THEY CAN'T THINK STRAIGHT!
FRAGGED OUT FRIG-BITCH!
SCAT, BOYS!
CAN'T MOVE!
GAS...
GLUE SHOOTERS!
...STUCK TO THE ROAD!
5

THE ACTIVISTS ORIGINATED AS A SKINHEAD CULT BUT UNDER THE LEADERSHIP OF BRANDON TOLSEN THEIR IRE WAS REDIRECTED AT THE NON-HUMAN SUJUL AND MANY NEW RECRUITS CAME FROM A DIVERSITY OF BACKGROUNDS — ALL FELT DISENFRANCHISED BY SOCIETY AT LARGE.
BEEN WATCHIN' YOU,
WORKIN' UP A SWEAT IN THAT WILD RIOT!
SO VIRILE!
AFTER THE RALLY DISINTEGRATED, BRANDON FLED DOWN AN ALLEY...
TRAGIC TRAVESTIES OF WOMEN, THAT'S ALL YOU ARE!
GOOD ENOUGH FOR YOU, MAN-MEAT!
THEY MELTED OUT OF THE SHADOWS, ATTACKING FROM ALL SIDES,
— IT WASN'T JUST THE OVERWHELMING NUMBERS,
— VENOMOUS TALONS, BURNING PAIN, CONFUSION, LOSS OF CO-ORDINATION, FOCUS! 6

BRANDON EVENTUALLY ESCAPED HIS TORMENTRESSES, BUT NOT BEFORE THEY'D HAD THEIR WAY WITH HIM. THE DELIRIOUS DREAMS BEGAN SHORTLY AFTERWARDS...

IN DR. BARBARA LINDEN'S SURGERY,

THOSE VIVID ANXIETY DREAMS, THEY FREQUENTLY OCCUR AFTER A MAN HAS EXPERIENCED GROUP SEX WITH SYRENS. - COULD ALSO BE A SIGN, BRANDON, THAT YOU'RE ESPECIALLY SUSCEPTIBLE TO THEIR SPECIALISED HORMONES, WHICH ARE CLEARLY WREAKING HAVOC WITHIN YOUR SYSTEM. AT THIS POINT, I CAN'T RULE OUT THE CHANCE THAT YOU MIGHT BE ONE OF THOSE RARE CASES WHO'LL UNDERGO A RAPID TRANSFORMATION.

JEZUZ! CAN YOU DO ANYTHING FOR ME, DOC? - STOP THOSE BLASTED VISIONS?

HARD TO SAY, BRANDON. YOU SEE, EACH INDIVIDUAL SYREN'S HORMONES ARE SLIGHTLY DIFFERENT. WHEN THEY ARE TRANSMITTED TO YOU DURING SEX THEY BOND TOGETHER, CREATE A NEW STRAIN. THAT'S WHY OUR MEDICAL TECHNOLOGY CAN'T KEEP UP.

IT'S THE KEY TO THE MUTATION OF A HUMAN MAN INTO A SYREN; IT'S HOW THEY EVOLVE, BECOME MORE HUMANLIKE AND DEVELOP A STRONGER RESISTANCE TO THE HUMAN IMMUNITY SYSTEM.

THEY ARE ACTUALLY JUST A REPRODUCTIVE SYSTEM. - A MIMIC!

THEY LOOK LIKE WOMEN YET THEY ARE NOT WOMEN — THEY'RE ARGUABLY NOT EVEN FEMALE! THESE CREATURES DO NOT POSSESS WOMBS, CANNOT CREATE LIFE! THEY DESTROY IN ORDER TO PERPETUATE THE SPECIES THROUGH MUTATION.

THE SYRENS ARE CREATED FROM MEN, FROM WHOSE REMAINS THEY RETAIN ANYTHING USEFUL — SKILLS, KNOWLEDGE, WHATEVER — DURING THE FINAL STAGES OF CONVERTING AND CONSUMING THEM.

ALL I CAN DO FOR YOU FOR NOW IS GIVE YOU SOME MEDICATION - IT COMES WITH A CAUTION — DON'T USE WITH STEROIDS.

...COULD HAVE THE OPPOSITE EFFECT!

DAMN!

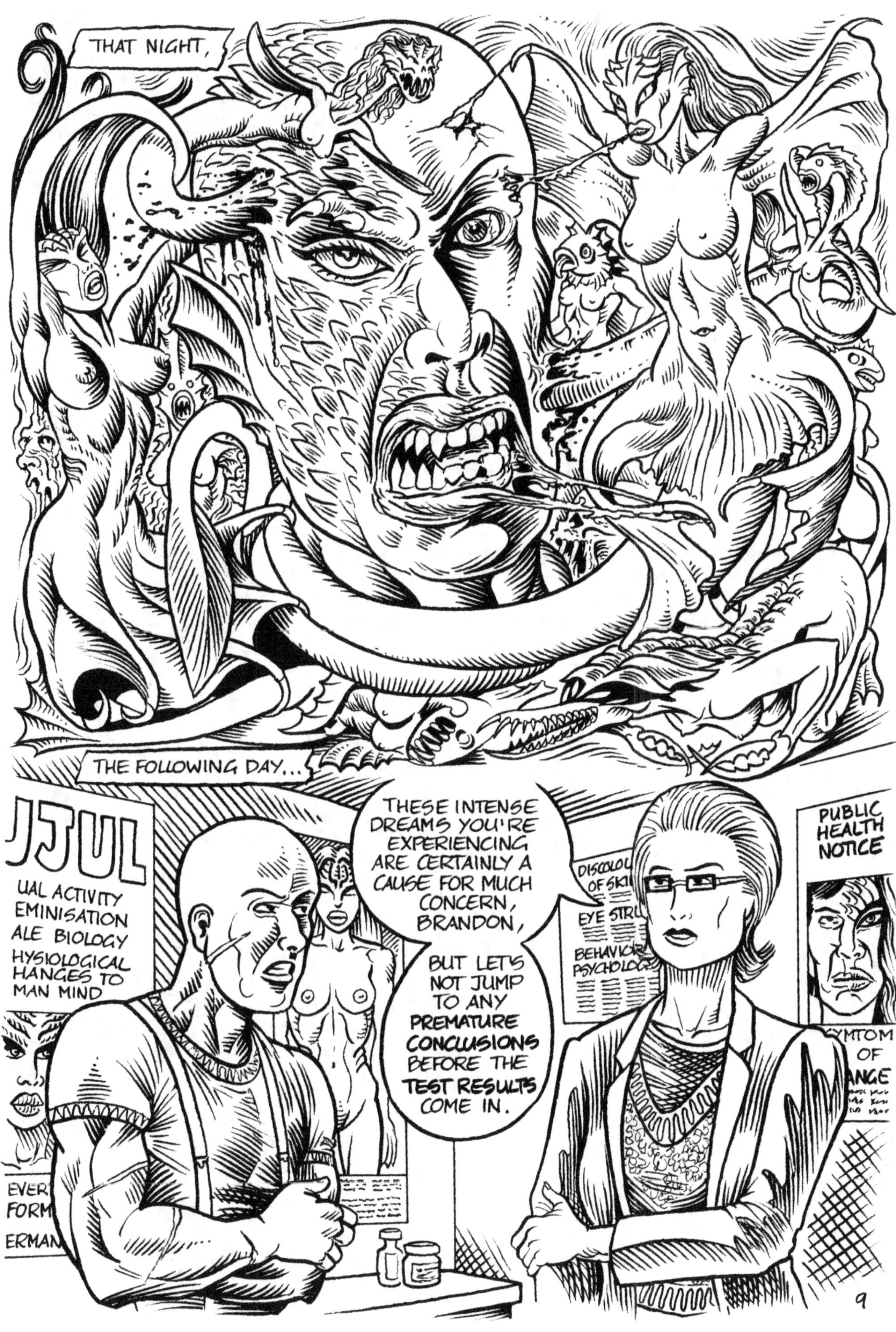
THAT NIGHT,

THE FOLLOWING DAY...

JJUL
UAL ACTIVITY
EMINISATION
ALE BIOLOGY
HYSIOLOGICAL
HANGES TO
MAN MIND

EVER
FORM
ERMAN

THESE INTENSE DREAMS YOU'RE EXPERIENCING ARE CERTAINLY A CAUSE FOR MUCH CONCERN, BRANDON,

BUT LET'S NOT JUMP TO ANY PREMATURE CONCLUSIONS BEFORE THE TEST RESULTS COME IN.

PUBLIC HEALTH NOTICE

DISCOLOU
OF SKI

EYE STRU

BEHAVIOR
PSYCHOLOG

YMTOM
OF
ANGE

9

... IN A SECRET MEETING BETWEEN REPRESENTATIVES OF THE PRIME MINISTER AND THE SUJUL ...
WE'RE PREPARED TO WORK OUT A MUTUALLY BENEFICIAL SOLUTION.
WE, THE SISTERHOOD OF THE SUJUL, ARE MORE THAN HAPPY TO MAKE YOUR DREAM OF A MUTUALLY BENEFICIAL CO-OPERATION BETWEEN OUR SPECIES A REALITY. BUT WE HAVE SPECIFIC REQUIREMENTS THAT ARE ABSOLUTELY CRUCIAL TO OUR CONTINUED SURVIVAL AS A SPECIES.
BEARING IN MIND WHAT KAVALU, OUR CLAN LEADER, HAS JUST TOLD YOU, THE SUJUL HAVE A PROPOSAL FOR YOU.
WE CAN USE YOUR UNDESIRABLES, THE SCUM - CRIMINALS, DRUG LORDS, SOCIAL MISFITS, MURDERERS, RAPISTS. ... TAKE THEM OFF THE STREETS, EASE THE PRESSURE ON YOUR PENAL SYSTEM.
HMMM, INTERESTING.
THE IDEA CERTAINLY DOES HAVE SOME MERIT.

THERE IS ALSO THE PROBLEM OF THOSE ACTIVISTS. THEY CAN BE LINKED TO THE MURDERS OF SUJUL. WITH ALL DUE RESPECT, YOUR PEACE-KEEPING AND JUDICIAL SYSTEM LEAVE SOMETHING TO BE DESIRED. TOO MANY OF THESE MISCREANTS ARE SLIPPING THROUGH YOUR NET!
WE CONCUR. THE ACTIVISTS ARE STIRRING UP TROUBLE, CREATING A LOT OF UNREST AND DISSENT.
NOT TO MENTION THE EFFECT ALL THIS IS HAVING ON POPULAR OPINION! THE OPPOSITION IS GAINING CREDIBILITY!
TOO TRUE, MY SAPIEN FRIENDS, AND I BELIEVE AN ELECTION IS DUE SOON. CAN'T HAVE THEM GETTING BACK IN, ...RUIN EVERYTHING!
YES, SOMETHING HAS TO BE DONE...
WE CAN DEAL WITH THE ACTIVISTS BUT IT'S BOUND TO BE MESSY! IN ANY EVENT, IF WE TAKE CARE OF IT, YOUR HANDS ARE CLEAN.
BUT TO DO THAT EFFICIENTLY WE NEED THE KIND OF WEAPONS THEY ARE USING AGAINST US — FIREARMS THAT YOU CAN SUPPLY.
GIVE US THOSE, WE'LL CLEAN THEM OUT, EASY!
I SEE...

11

LATER THAT WEEK,
HEY, BRANDON! HOW ARE YOU?
FINE, SHARA, YOURSELF?
BUSY! CIVIL DEFENCE'S GOT US ALL ON DOUBLE ROSTERS. MISSING PERSONS CASES.
THEY'RE MOUNTING UP...
BET THEY ARE! SPEAKIN' OF MISSIN' PERSONS, NEARLY BECAME ONE...
GOT AMBUSHED BY A PACK OF SWAMPIES AFTER THAT FRACAS OF A RALLY.
CUT YOU UP SOME, BY THE LOOK OF YOU. THAT ALL THEY DID?
AFRAID NOT. THEY SWARMED ME, AND DID ME. DON'T KNOW HOW MANY, MORE THAN TEN...
SHIT!
YOU GO SEE A QUACK? YOU GONNA BE OKAY?
DUNNO. WAITIN' FOR TEST RESULTS.
WHAT'S GOING TO BECOME OF THE ACTION WE'VE BEEN PLANNING FOR MONTHS, NOW?
NO CHANGE. STILL GOING AHEAD THIS WEEKEND. BE THERE!

LIKE SOME OTHERS IN THE CIVIL DEFENCE UNIT, SHARA CLAINE MOONLIGHTED WITH THE ACTIVISTS DURING SOME OF THEIR METICULOUSLY PLANNED ACTIONS. HER YOUNGER BROTHER HAD BEEN SNATCHED BY SUJUL AND NEVER SEEN AGAIN. SINCE THEN, SHARA HAD HARBOURED AN INTENSE LOATHING OF SUJUL.
THIS IS THE DAY. WE'VE BEEN PREPARING FOR THIS ACTION FOR MONTHS. THERE'S SCORES OF SWAMPIES HIDIN' OUT, OUT HERE!
THAT'S ONE VAST VALLEY!
HELL OF A TERRITORY TO COVER.
TAKE US MORE THAN A DAY!
WE HAVE THE ENTIRE LONG WEEKEND. THIS TIME, WE MUST FIND THEIR DEN, AS WELL AS ANY RECENT MISSING PERSONS – IF THEY'RE STILL HUMAN.

IN THE VALLEY,
THUP!
ZIP!
SNIPERS!
UNDER COVER, SAJA, NOW!
IT'S SWAMPIES! — WITH MILITARY ISSUE FIREARMS!
SPOTTED ONE JUST DOWN THERE, NEAR THAT KNOLL!
WHERE AND HOW DID THOSE FISH-HAGS GET THOSE KIND OF ARMS?

WHERE ARE THEY, KULVA? CAN YOU SEE THEM?
NO, TRIVAVE. THEY'VE SCATTERED.
BUT WE HAVE TO FIND THEM ALL. THEY'VE COME TO KILL US.
WE HAVE NO CHOICE BUT TO KILL THEM
PITY. A DEAD MAN IS ONE LESS SUJUL AND A WASTE OF VITAL SKILLS WE MIGHT HAVE ACQUIRED, USED.
ELSEWHERE IN THE WOODS...
THE BITCHIN' THINGS MIGHT HAVE ATTAINED HIGH TECH WEAPONS,
BUT THEY'VE GOT NO IDEA HOW TO USE THEM!

THAT BITCHIN' SWAMPY DISAPPEARED 'ROUND THE FAR SIDE OF THIS MASSIVE OUTCROP...
THIS'S TURNED INTO A GODDAM' FIASCO!
THE CONFLICT HAD SPREAD WIDE THROUGHOUT THE FOREST, WITH SMALL GROUPS AND INDIVIDUALS STALKING ONE ANOTHER...
...GOD KNOWS WHAT'S HAPPENED TO THE CREW! WE HAVE TO RE-GROUP, OR ELSE!...
?!

16

BITCHIN' FREAKS!
THEY'RE EVERYWHERE!
GOD KNOWS HOW MANY THERE ARE OUT HERE!
CAN'T SEE A SIGN OF ANYONE BUT I CAN HEAR THE FIGHTING...
SCANT FEW IN THIS RESISTANCE GROUP HAVE THE DISCIPLINE OF THE C.D.U.
THAT'S WHY THIS ACTION HAS TURNED INTO A SHAMBLES UNDER THE FIRST SIGN OF PRESSURE!
MOST OF THEM ARE JUST RABBLE! IF IT WASN'T FOR BRANDON, I'D NEVER HAVE JOINED UP WITH THEM.
AS THE LEADER OF THIS CELL, BRANDON DID HIS BEST TO INSTILL FOCUS AND A SENSE OF PURPOSE AMONG THESE THUGS!
UNLIKE MOST OF THEM, HE ACTUALLY GIVES A DAMN!
17

S. CARTER
2 0 0 9

IT'S MADNESS! I'M HAVING THESE VISIONS WHILE WIDE AWAKE!
...IN BROAD DAYLIGHT!
NO MAN IS IMMUNE. THE EXPERIENCE DIFFERS SUBSTANTIALLY AMONG INDIVIDUALS. FOR A FEW, SEVERAL YEARS MIGHT PASS BEFORE ANY CHANGE OCCURS...
FOR MANY, THE PROCESS IS A GRADUAL ONE, OCCURRING OVER MANY WEEKS, OR EVEN MONTHS,
AND FOR A RARE FEW ESPECIALLY UNFORTUNATE MEN, IT CAN HAPPEN QUICKLY — SUDDENLY!
BUT IN THE END, THE SUJUL'S VIRAL HORMONES WIN.
NO! IT CAN'T BE!
TELL ME IT'S JUST ANOTHER VISION!
BRANDON TOLSEN!
— THAT WAS HIS NAME,
WHO HE WAS.
FOR ANY MAN WHO HAS SEXUAL RELATIONS WITH THE SUJUL JUST ONE TOO MANY TIMES, THE ULTIMATE CONSEQUENCES ARE INEVITABLE.
...FOR SOME MEN, ONLY ONE SEXUAL ENCOUNTER IS ONE TOO MANY!
19

BRANDON TOLSEN HAD REACHED THE POINT OF NO RETURN – SUJULAH – AS THE SUJUL KNEW IT. THE MOMENT WHEN THE MAN NO LONGER EXISTS AND A SUJUL HAS REPLACED HIM, BODY AND SOUL.
THE SUJUL VIRAL HORMONE CARRIES THEIR ENTIRE GENETIC HISTORY AND CODE, WHICH ARE IMPRINTED UPON THE VICTIM'S BRAIN AND MANIFEST IN THE FORM OF HALLUCINATORY EPISODES – A PRELUDE TO HIS FATAL TRANSFORMATION.
I AM BORN, HE IS GONE.
HIS MEMORY, KNOWLEDGE, SKILLS AND EXPERIENCE ARE MINE, NOW. I KNOW HIS LANGUAGE, HIS WORLD AND HIS KIN.
I KNOW HIM INTIMATELY.
AND I KNOW WHAT I AM BECAUSE HE KNEW MANY JUST LIKE ME.
BUT I AM ME AND I AM NEW. I MUST FIND THOSE WHO ARE LIKE ME. – RUSULKA, SYRENS, SWAMPIES –
THAT'S WHAT BRANDON TOLSEN CALLED US! BUT THE TRUE NAME IS SUJUL. HE HATED US – THE SUJUL.
HE WAS AN ACTIVIST WAGING A WAR AGAINST US – A CAUSE THAT CONSUMED HIM!
YET BUT FOR HIM, I WOULD NOT BE HERE!
KOOM!
YET ANOTHER ONE OF THE HIDEOUS THINGS!
BUSH'S CRAWLIN' WITH 'EM!
...BLOW HER BRAINS OUT!

MOMENTS AFTER SHE SHOT THE SUJUL, SHARA FOUND TWO OF THE CREW,
JUST LOOK AT IT, LYING THERE! NAKED, LEWD, DISGUSTING!
VILE, DESPICABLE CREATURES! JUST WHAT ARE THEY, ANYWAY? WHERE'D THEY COME FROM?
THE SEA. THEY'RE ANCIENT. —STORY IS, THEIR SWARMING HORDES SWALLOWED UP ENTIRE RACES OF MAN IN AN AGE B'FORE THE DAWN OF CIVILISATION AS WE KNOW IT...
SHARA! YOU HAVE TO COME, SEE THIS!
—BACK ALONG THIS TRAIL A BIT.
...BRANDON'S CLOTHES AND WEAPON — LYIN' IN A POOL OF STINKIN' OOZE!
SCAZ ©2009

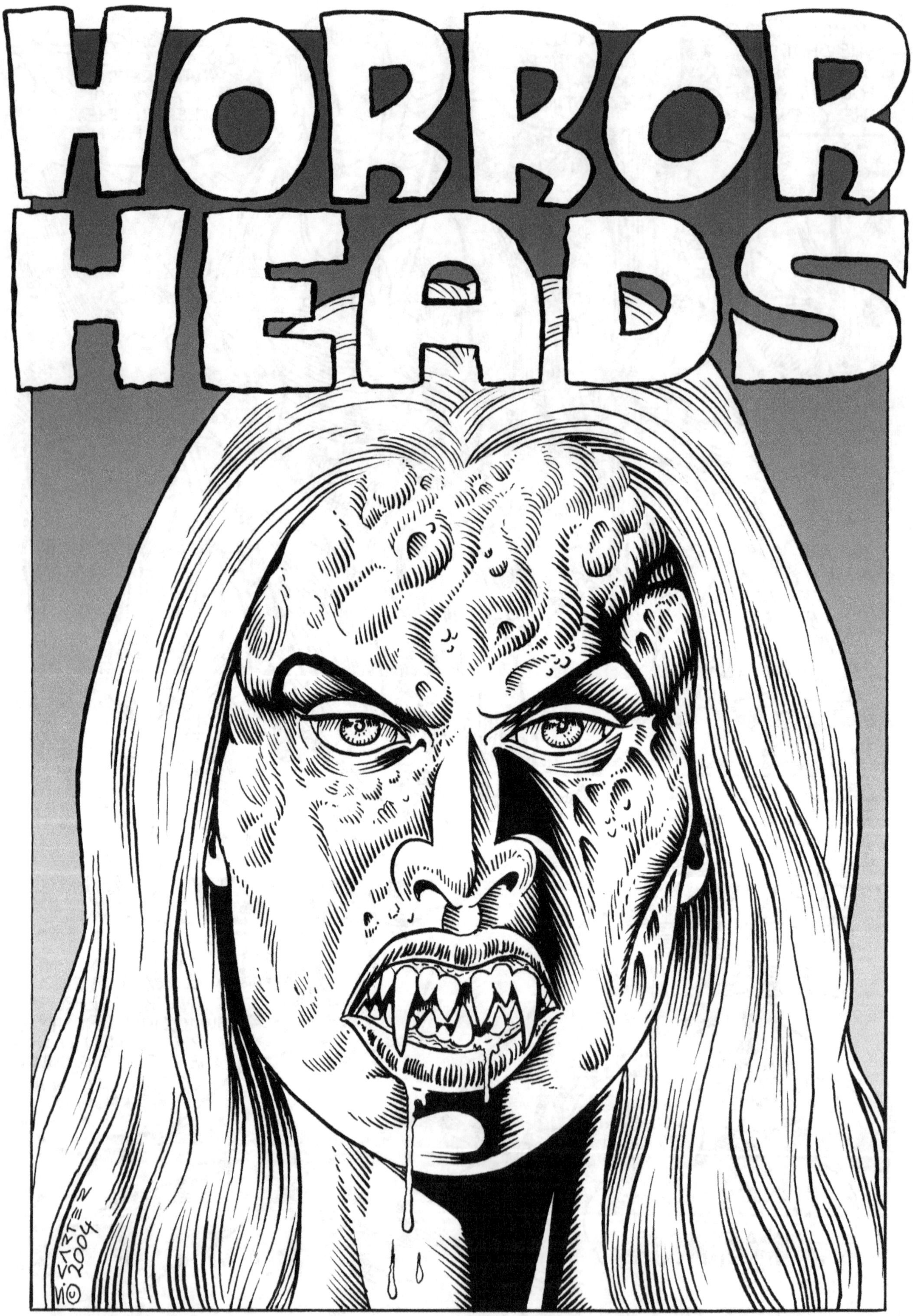

HORROR HEADS

WAR SHOULD ALWAYS BE THE LAST ALTERNATIVE; THOUGH MANY ARE LOATH TO ADMIT IT, OFTEN THERE IS NO ALTERNATIVE.
THIS WAR IS NOT GOING TO END SOON. THE SIMPLE FACT IS THAT WARS ARE NEVER SHORT.
I

BEING THAT THIS ONE IS FINANCED BY ONE OF THE LARGEST MULTINATIONALS ON THE GLOBE, IT IS NOT A POPULAR WAR. THERE ARE PLENTY OF DETRACTORS,
...AND DARE I SAY IT, THE MAJORITY OF THEM ARE ILL INFORMED. NO DOUBT, MOST OF THEM SIMPLY WANT TO BE SEEN TO BE FOLLOWING A POPULAR CAUSE, REGARDLESS OF THE FACTS...
II

THE ENEMY IS COMPLETELY DEVOTED TO ITS CAUSE. NO ROOM FOR DEBATE; ROOM ONLY FOR ONE VICTOR.
FOR THE SAKE OF HUMANITY THAT VICTOR MUST BE US!
CO-EXISTENCE IS NOT AN OPTION
...I CAN TELL YOU THAT THE ROOTS OF THIS CONFLICT ORIGINATED WAY BACK IN THE PAST ~ BUT WHERE TO ASSIGN THE BLAME? THAT QUESTION I CANNOT ANSWER.
III

HOW LONG HAVE I BEEN INCOLVED IN THIS? IT BEGAN FOR ME AT A TIME WELL BEFORE MOST OF US HAD EVEN REALISED THAT THE COURSE TOWARDS WHOLESALE WARFARE HAD ALREADY BEEN SET INTO MOTION...
...THE FIRST MAJOR ATTACK ON A CITY HADN'T YET OCCURRED
FOR A LONG TIME, THERE EXISTED THE ISSUE OF HOSTILE OUTSIDER CLANS. THEIR NUMBERS WERE STEADILY INCREASING, SMALLER GROUPS AMALGAMATED INTO LARGER, COMPLEXLY ORGANISED NETWORKS.
SIX YEARS AGO, I WAS IN TRANSIT BETWEEN TWO CITIES, HAD NO COMPREHENSION OF JUST HOW DRASTICALLY THINGS WERE ABOUT TO CHANGE...
IV

HORROR HEADS
GOT TO ADMIT, CENTURIES OF ENVIRONMENTAL ABUSE AND NEGLECT BY THE MASSIVE MULTINATIONALS HAS CERTAINLY TRANSFORMED OUR WORLD...
YOU'RE NOT WRONG ABOUT THAT, FRIEND.
DON'T FORGET THE COUNTLESS IRRESPONSIBLE EXPERIMENTS IN GENE MANIPULATION BY THE BIG PHARMACEUTICAL CONGLOMETRATES ~ THEY HAD A PART TO PLAY.
ONE LOOK OUT THE WINDOW'S A STARK REMINDER OF THAT.
...YEAH, SEE WHAT YOU MEAN...
THAT'S THE BIGGEST HIPPIG I'VE EVER SEEN!
THEN YOU AIN'T SEEN NUTHIN' ...THEY GET A LOT BIGGER THAN THAT!
S. CARTER AND A. RYDYR © 1999 - 2005

IT'S A WEIRD THING, Y'KNOW - I MEAN, WHO'D HAVE EVER IMAGINED THAT WE'D INHERIT A WORLD IN WHICH PIGS MIGHT FLY!
GAWD! WISH THOSE TWO'D JUST SHUT UP!
...BEEN AT IT ALL DAY!
THERE'S NOT A SPECIES OF FLORA OR FAUNA OUT HERE THAT DOESN'T OWE ITS ORIGIN TO SOME LEVEL OF GENETIC TAMPERING!
...TRIP'S LONG AN' AGONISIN' ENOUGH AS IT IS!
...AND ALL SUPPOSEDLY FOR THE BENEFIT OF HUMANKIND.
MORE LIKE BIG PROFITS, WHICH ARE USED TO BUY OFF PUPPET POLITICIANS AND A CORRUPT SELF-SERVING SYSTEM.
THERE IT IS! I KNEW THAT ROADTRAIN'D BE OUT HERE SOMEWHERE. TRYIN' TO TRICK US AGAIN BY TAKIN' A DIF'RENT ROUTE.

WHAT D'YOU S'POSE THAT IS? IT'S BIG 'N' IT'S COMIN' OUR WAY...
!?
...I HOPE IT'S NOT WHAT I THINK IT IS...
AN' WHAT WOULD THAT BE...?

HORROR HEADS! TRIBES OF MUTANT AMAZONS...
WORD IS THEY'RE NOW GATHERING TOGETHER IN BIG NUMBERS AND RECENTLY, HORDES OF THEM HAVE BEEN ATTACKING ROAD TRAINS.
EVERYBODY! GET IN YOUR SEATS - BUCKLE UP - WE ARE UNDER ATTACK!
SECURITY! MAN YOUR POSTS!
THEY'RE USING THOSE MASSIVE BEASTS TO RAM US - SMASH US!
TAKING EVASIVE ACTION NOW!
HOLD TIGHT!

GOT THE BITCH!
THAK! THAK!
...HAD NO IDEA THEY WERE SO UGLY!
YEP! THAT'S WHY THEY'RE CALLED HORROR HEADS.
THUT!
AN EXCELLENT SHOT! AN' SHE'S SUCH A PRETTY ONE AT THAT! HEH! HEH! HEH!
YEAH! PRETTY AS A PICTURE!
KU-RASCH!
DON'T FERGET, WE WANT 'EM ALIVE! WE NEED LABOURERS, BREEDERS...

ROUND THEM UP!
...ANY ESCAPE, YOU WILL BE BEATEN.
PLENTY OF BOYS 'N' MEN!
YEAH! PITY MOST OF THEM 'R' EITHER WASTED OLD GEEPS,
...OR PUSSY WHIPPED PANTY-WASTE WIMPS!
MY FATHER'S THE MANAGIN' DIRECTOR OF TRANSNATION ROAD TRAINS, SO HANG IN THERE. WE'LL GET OUT OF THIS...
YEAH, RIGHT! MAKES ME FEEL REAL SAFE, NOW!
TOLD YOU TO SHUT THAT THING UP!
PLEASE, HE'S JUST A BABY.
...AN' YOU THINK JUS' 'CAUSE YER POPPED A HATCHLIN' OF YER OWN YER SOMETHIN' SPECIAL, EH?
VERMIN LIKE RATS 'N' RABBITS BIN DOIN' THAT FER AGES. ...MEANS NUTHIN'.
WAH!

NO! STOP!
WAH!
THERE'LL BE NO MORE SQUAWKIN! MY LITTLE MEAT MAGGOT!
SPTHAKK!
STOP THAT PATHETIC CATERWAULIN', YOU SILLY COW! YER WELL ENOUGH EQUIPPED TO HAVE ANOTHER SPROGLET ANYWAYS!
CAN'T JUS' SIT HERE AND NOT DO ANYTHING!
WAHGH!
HIDEOUS INHUMAN HAG!
FUMP!
SO! THE INDIGNANT LITTLE BOY WANTS TO PLAY AT BEING A BIG SELF-RIGHTEOUS MAN, EH!
TIE HIM TIGHT!

CONSIDER YERSELF A BIG BRAVE VIRILE MAN, EH? IT'S TIME TO SEE JUST HOW MANLY YOU ARE...
MAKE IT GOOD, OR IT'S THE CORPSE PILE FOR YOU.
SILLY BASTARD! SET HIMSELF RIGHT UP FOR THAT ONE - STILL, PITY ANY LAD THOSE THINGS FANCY...
YEAH, REAL BEAUTY QUEENS, EVERY ONE.
THESE TROLL DOLLS THINK THEY'RE GOD'S GIFT TO MEN, BELIEVE IT!
...AN' THEY'RE EVEN CRAZIER THAN THEY'RE UGLY!
SHUT UP, YOU PIECES OF SHIT!
THIS ISN'T GOOD, BOY!
I'M NOT IMPRESSED.
CAN'T FEEL A THING.
...AN' WE BIN AT IT FOR A WHILE, NOW.
...YOU GOT ANOTHER MINUTE, BOY.
...YOU A MAN OR NOT?
WHAT CAN I SAY? YOU'RE OBVIOUSLY NOT MY TYPE. I PREFER WOMEN...
YER GONNA BE REAL SORRY YER SAID THAT, BOY!

YER EITHER VERY BRAVE OR INCREDIBLY STUPID!
HE'S AN *IDGIT!* WHAT'D YOU EXPECT FROM THE SON OF THE MANAGING DIRECTOR OF *TRANSNATION ROAD TRAINS?*
SHOULD 'A PUMPED 'ER FOR ALL YOU'RE WORTH! NOW, WE'RE ALL IN THE *SHIT!*
THE OLD GIMPS CAN GO WITH THE REST OF THE LABOURERS. SEND THE OTHER MEN TO THE *BREEDING BARRACKS* AND CLEAN THEM UP,
...EXCEPT FOR *HIM!*

ALRIGHT, WE'RE HERE! THERE'S A SETTLEMENT OF HORROR HEADS NEARBY, AS YOU KNOW, SO MAINTAIN HIGH ALERT STATUS!
OUR MISSION IS TO ESTABLISH WHETHER OR NOT THE MANAGING DIRECTOR'S SON IS STILL ALIVE AND IF SO, LOCATE HIM, ALONG WITH ANY OTHER SURVIVORS.
WE HAVE THE OPTION OF ATTEMPTING A RESCUE OP ONLY IF THE RISKS ARE MINIMAL.
HOWEVER, WE MUST REMAIN FOCUSED. OUR PRIMARY OBJECTIVE IS TO GATHER STRATEGIC INFORMATION!
ONLY REASON WE'RE OUT HERE IS 'CAUSE THIS TIME, THAT PRAT JUS' 'APPENED TO BE ON THE LAST ROAD TRAIN THAT WENT MISSIN'.
...THAT 'N' THE FACT THE COST OF LOSIN' ALL THOSE ROAD TRAINS IS STARTIN' TO MOUNT UP...
...'N' THE SLACK SHITS'VE REALISED THEY'VE GOTTA GET OFF THEIR ARSES 'N' DO SOMETHIN'.

THERE WERE A HELL OF A LOT OF 'EM. TRACKS 'N' DRAG MARKS EVERYWHERE. SOME PRETTY LARGE BEASTS WITH 'EM TOO! ...AT LEAST TWO DIF'RENT TYPES. ...MADE NO SECRET OF WHERE THEY WERE HEADED, EITHER.

THAT'S ONE BIG VILLAGE, TOO BIG FOR US TO TAKE ON...
THAT PRAT, IF HE'S ALIVE, 'LL BE IN THERE, SOMEWHERE.
TAKE A LOOK AT WHAT'S LYING IN THAT PEN DOWN THERE!
...IT'S A SALVAGER'S GOLDMINE!
...I'M FOR GOIN' DOWN 'N' GETTIN' A CLOSER LOOK.
...'N' OVER THERE, IN THAT LABOUR CAMP - IF YOU COULD CALL IT THAT - ARE WHAT'S LEFT OF WHAT HAS TO BE THE FORMER OCCUPANTS OF THOSE ROAD TRAINS...
CONDITIONS DOWN THERE MAKE THE WAGE SYSTEMS OF THE MULTINATIONALS SEEM ALMOST HUMANE...
BUT I CAN'T SEE ANY SIGN OF THAT PRAT WE'RE MEANT TO FIND AMONG THEM...

AREN'T THESE THE BEASTS THEY USE TO RAM THE ROAD TRAINS?
THEY ARE BUT THEY'RE NOT NORMALLY DANGEROUS, UNLESS YOU THREATEN OR STARTLE THEM AND RIGHT NOW THEY MAKE PERFECT COVER...
OKAY, COAST IS CLEAR. WE CAN MAKE IT RIGHT UP TO THE ENCLOSURE THIS TIME.
LET'S GO, QUICKLY, NOW!
...UP 'N' OVER BEFORE ANYONE SEES...
QUITE A COLLECTION!
COULD SALVAGE TOGETHER AT LEAST ONE GOOD RIG OUT OF THIS LOT...
BET THAT'S JUST WHAT THEY'RE DOIN'.
...APPEARS WE'VE GOT A PRETTY MUCH ROADWORTHY ONE HERE,
...COULD BE USEFUL.
...AND IT COMES COMPLETE WITH A CHARGED UP POWER UNIT!
HUH?
PSST, YOU TWO! YOU'VE GOT TO SEE THIS!
THIS WAY... BE QUIET.

MOVE THAT ARSE, BOY!
CRRAK!
SOUNDS LIKE QUITE A PARTY RAGIN' ON JUS' UP 'ERE!
KEEP QUIET 'N' KEEP LOW 'N' DON'T EVEN THINK ABOUT LIGHTIN' THAT CIGARETTE...
THINK YOU'VE SEEN IT ALL? THEN TAKE A PEEK THROUGH THERE...
FASTER, MY HUMAN MAN MAGGOT!
YOU'D BETTER NOT LOSE THIS TIME!
PLEASE TELL ME THERE'S AN END TO THIS!
NO ESCAPE, BUDDY! THIS IS THE END OF THE LINE...
WELCOME TO HELL!
C'MON! ONLY FIVE LAPS TO GO!
DON'T YOU DARE SLACKEN OFF NOW!

THE GRUB PIT RACES ARE MY FAVOURITE!
I REALLY LIKE THAT PALE ONE! HE'S SO WHITE!
...AND THE WAY HE WRIGGLES HIS STUMPS GETS ME ALL EXCITED!
YOU CAN HAVE HIM FIRST, IF YOU WANT, MAHDU. BUT ONLY IF YOU DON'T COMPLAIN WHEN IT COMES TIME TO SHARE HIM AROUND... ...REMEMBER NOW, THEY BELONG TO ALL OF US!
SO, WHO'S YOUR FAVOURITE AUNTY THEN, MAHDU?
YOU ARE, AUNTY ANGARA!
AND WHY IS THAT, MY PET?
'CAUSE YOU LET ME PLAY WITH MEN JUS' LIKE OLDER GIRLS DO, EVEN THOUGH I'M NOT REALLY OLD ENOUGH TO YET...
YOU'RE SUCH A CLEVER LITTLE GIRL! THAT'S RIGHT ~ THE EARLIER YOU LEARN, THE SMARTER YOU GET AND THE FASTER YOU GET AHEAD. IT'S THE QUICK OR THE DEAD! ONLY THE CLEVER ONES GET TO LIVE A LONG, HAPPY LIFE!
ERK! DON'T LIKE HIM!
...HE'S ALL SPACKY 'N' SLUGGY! BET I CAN HIT HIM IN THE HEAD!
THATTA GIRL, MAHDU! THROW YOUR SCRAPS INTO THE GRUB PIT. GOT TO KEEP 'EM WELL FED!
WHUCK!!
I'VE NEVER SEEN SUCH OBSCENE CRUELTY! IT'S COMPLETELY PERVERSE!
THEY ARE TRULY A RETROGRADED, DEGENERATE BREED!
...FIRST TIME I'VE SEEN IT BUT I'VE HEARD OF IT. CALLED THE GRUB PIT ~ A FATE RESERVED FOR MEN WHO INCUR THE CHIEFTESS' DISPLEASURE!
13

NO WONDER PEOPLE REFUSE TO ACCEPT THAT THESE FREAKS ARE ACTUALLY RELATED TO THE HUMAN RACE!
YES, SAD BUT TRUE. TWISTED BY COUNTLESS GENERATIONS OF MUTATION THEY INDEED ARE BUT THERE'S STILL A GENETIC LINK BETWEEN US AND THEM.
THEIR MALES ARE PATHETIC PUNY THINGS, BORN STERILE AND IMPOTENT, LIVE LITTLE MORE THAN ELEVEN OR TWELVE YEARS.
...BUT WHILE THERE ARE HUMANS AVAILABLE FOR THEM TO ABDUCT AND ENSLAVE, THEY'LL CONTINUE TO BREED...
HEY, LOOK! THAT'S HIM!
YOU SURE? I CAN'T TELL FROM HERE...
NO, SHE'S RIGHT! IT IS HIM!
14

HOW CRUEL IS FATE? THE SON OF THE MANAGING DIRECTOR OF TRANSNATION ROAD TRAINS WINDS UP IN A GODDAMNED GRUB PIT!
...IN ANY CASE, NO ONE DESERVES WHAT THESE MUTANTS HAVE DONE TO HIM!
...NO MATTER WHO THEY ARE OR WHAT THEY MAY HAVE DONE.
YEAH, I HEAR YOU!
WE'VE FOUND WHAT WE CAME FOR AND I'VE SEEN ENOUGH! LET'S GO!
WE'RE NOT EVEN GONNA TRY AN' SAVE WHAT'S LEFT OF THE SORROWFUL LAD?
WHAT'S THE POINT?
!
?
FALL BACK! WE HAVE TO ASSESS THIS SITUATION CAREFULLY.
SHIT!
WE'VE BEEN MADE!
15

TAKE THEM OUT!
QUICK!
KLAT!
CUT THAT DUMB HUMAN TRAMP, DRESCHIA! CUT THE SLUT GOOD, NOW!
...ENTIRE CLAN'S GONNA BE BREATHIN' DOWN OUR BACKS IN NO TIME FLAT!
SSSSSSS!
ZZT!
AEIK!
ZZRK!
SLISH!
HERE THEY COME! HOW 'R' WE GONNA GET OUT OF THIS ONE?
I HAVE AN IDEA...

YOU'D BETTER KNOW WHAT YOU'RE DOIN'...
WE'VE BARELY A SECOND TO SPARE.
WE'VE GOTTA GET BACK OUT ON THE FAR SIDE OF THOSE HUGE BEASTS, AND FAST!
NOW! SET YOUR WEAPONS ON MILD...
GET THESE BEASTS MOVING...
STRAIGHT INTO THAT VILLAGE!
GRH!
THEY'VE CAUSED A STAMPEDE!
THE HUMIE SCUM ARE USIN' MOLECULAR MELTERS AND LASER CUTTERS, WHIPPIN' THE BEASTS INTO A FRENZY.
BREAK OUT THE POWER WEAPONS.

ZIP!
ZZRAK!
INCREASE THE VOLTAGE OF YOUR SHOCK LASHES.
...ONLY WAY TO GET THROUGH TO THEIR TINY BRAINS!
IF WE INTEND TO RESCUE THE TORSO KID, NOW'S THE PERFECT TIME...
FINE BY ME...
...SOUNDS LIKE THIS VILLAGE IS UNDER ATTACK!
THAT'S THE HISS OF A HEAT RAY!
...COULD WELL BE OUR TICKET OUT OF HERE...
HOPE YOU'RE RIGHT!
NEVER MIND WHAT'S GOIN' ON OUT THERE! IT'S OF NO CONCERN FOR YOU WRETCHED BITCHES!
GET BACK TO WORK!
YOU'RE CRAZY! WE JUS' GOT OUT OF THERE BY THE SKIN OF OUR TEETH,
...AN' NOW, YOU WANNA GO STRAIGHT BACK IN...
18

FOR CHRISSAKES! STOP WRIGGLING!
GET INTO THAT ROAD TRAIN YARD!
...WE'RE FIRIN' UP A RIG!
SHRIZZS!
NO WAY YOU'RE KEEPIN' ANY OF US IN THIS SWEAT SHOP A MINUTE LONGER, YOU MUTANT HARRIDAN!
YER GONNA DIE FER THIS HUMAN COW!
THAT'S IT, GIRL! THROTTLE THE HIDEOUS FREAK!
IT'S TOTAL CHAOS OUT THERE!
SCIISST!
SLAG!
FZSHT!
ZFT!

PLEASE! YOU HAVE TO TAKE US WITH YOU!
GET IN, QUICK! AN' HOLD TIGHT!
C'MON GET THIS HULK MOVIN'!
THEY'RE RIGHT WITH US!
...COMIN' AT US ON THE GROUND AND FROM THE AIR...
...AND THEY'RE WELL ARMED!
THE TORSO KID'S FLIPPIN' ABOUT LIKE AN EPILEPTIC!
STUMPS'LL BE JUST FINE, NOW.
...SOMEBODY DO SOMETHIN'!
WAK!
20

GOT A HANDY GUN? WANNA HELP,
'FRAID NOT,
SO GET DOWN!
GOT YOU NOW, FREAK-HAG!
YOU'RE COMIN' DOWN!
...INCOMING LASER CUTTER.
SLICIN' STRAIGHT THROUGH THE HULL!
AAIEGH!
ZCHL'IZ

ZZZRT!

JEZUZ! ...WHAT ARE HER CHANCES?
NOT GOOD.
IT'S ALL I CAN DO IF SHE'S TO HAVE ANY HOPE AT ALL.
SHE'S OUT COLD.
SSSSS
SHE'LL COME BACK 'ROUND SOON ENOUGH.

THE HAGS HAVE FLED. WE'RE FINALLY IN THE CLEAR.
GOTTA GET BACK FAST. GOT A LADY BACK THERE IN NEED OF A HOSPITAL.
TELL ME THIS IS NOT HAPPENING.
GOT SOME PAIN KILLERS HERE...

...SIX MONTHS LATER...
I SEE YOU'RE ON YOUR FEET AGAIN.
WHAT DO YOU THINK? I OPTED FOR THESE RATHER THAN THE SYNTHETI-ORGANICS... FULLY INTEGRATED, THRICE THE POWER.
YEAH, SUITS YOU.
...VERY IMPRESSIVE.
I INVITED YOU HERE TO THANK YOU FOR SAVING MY LIFE, ALONG WITH THOSE OF THE OTHERS, AND ALSO TO OFFER YOU A PERMANENT POSITION WITHIN THIS COMPANY.
AND THAT BEING?
I'M PUTTING TOGETHER A STRIKE FORCE
...THOSE MUTANT CLANS ARE BECOMING A SIGNIFICANT PROBLEM FOR EVERYBODY!
YOU THREE'D BE A GREAT ASSET, AND I PROMISE YOU FULL AUTONOMY IN ALL OPERATIONS...
WHEN DO WE START?
THE SOONER THE BETTER.

THE CONVERSATION ABRUPTLY CEASED AT THE SUDDEN ENTRANCE OF ANOTHER VISITOR,
I'LL GET STRAIGHT TO THE POINT...
I'M AWARE OF THIS STRIKE FORCE YOU'RE CREATIN'...
JUS' TELL ME WHERE I SIGN UP.
I WANT IN.
I'LL BE DAMNED!
IF YOU GOT WHAT IT TAKES, YOU'RE IN, LADY...
SCAR
2000/05

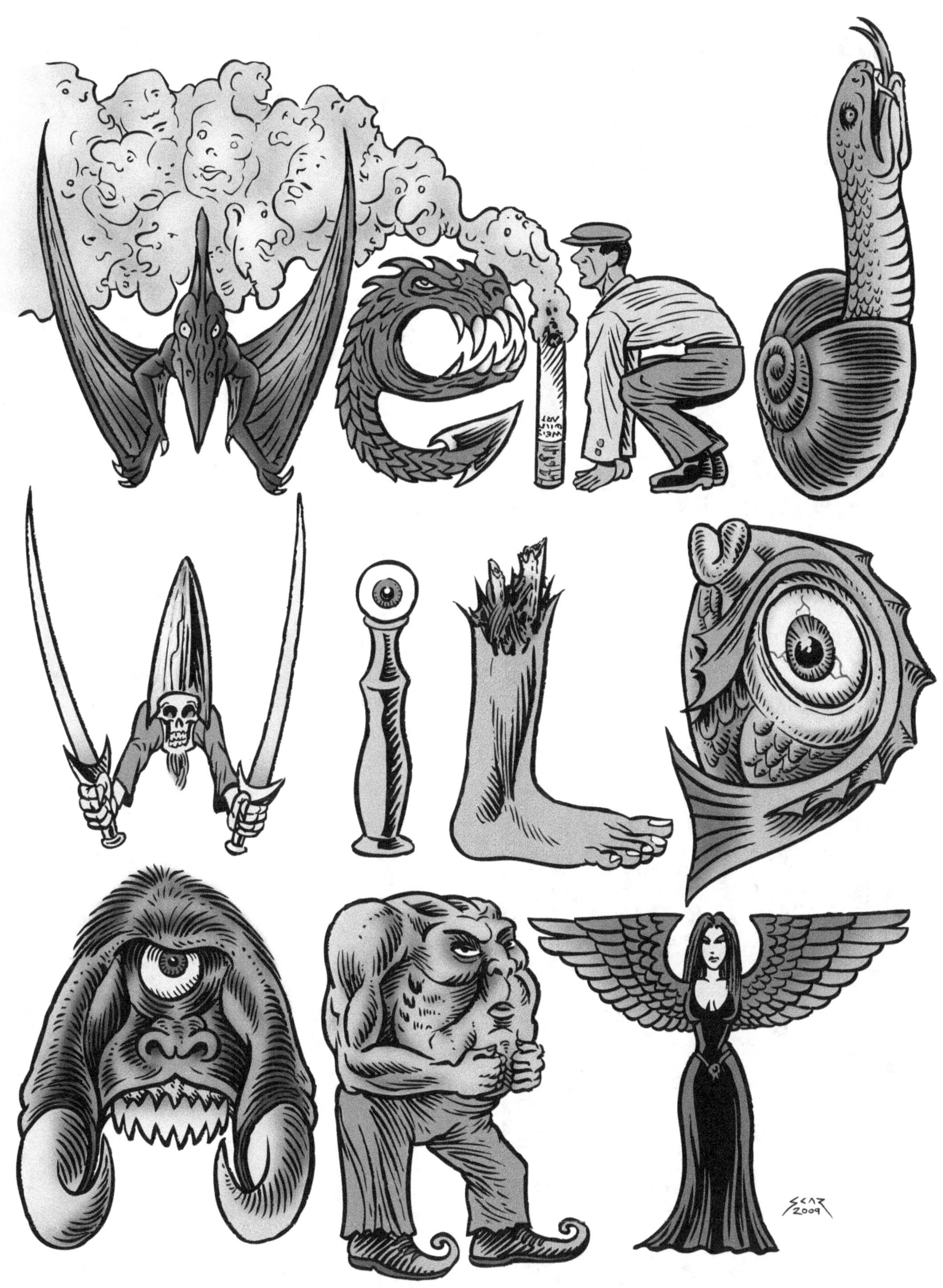

If you enjoyed this book by SCAR, have a look at their other titles and please consider writing a review. Thanks!

MORE BOOKS BY S.C.A.R.

Savage Bitch: ISBN 978-0987622907
Phantastique: ISBN 978-0987622938

Weird Worlds: ISBN 978-0987622914
Fantastique: ISBN 978-0987622921

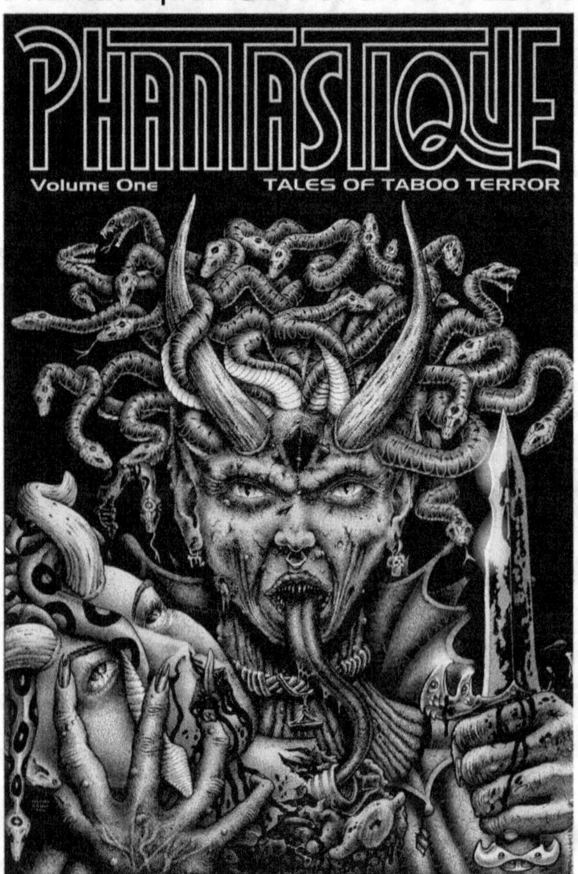

www.weirdwildart.com

CARTER RYDYR AND ETHAN SOMERVILLE
WEIRD WILD WEST
PART 1 – HELL DORADO
PART 2 – THE GOOD, THE BAD AND THE ZOMBIE

WEIRD WILD WEST

A New Novel by
Carter Rydyr
Ethan Somerville

Imagine a wild west that isn't just full of cowboys and outlaws, saloon girls and gamblers. Imagine a wild west that isn't just cacti, tumbleweeds and rolling desert as far as the eye can see. Imagine a wild west of mechanical horses, mutant killer plants, flying dinosaurs, headless indians and fearsome zombie gunslingers hell-bent on revenge.

Imagine the Weird Wild West.

Six colourful characters, some not entirely human, embark on a perilous journey south from Sunbleached Plains to Kellyville. A dapper dentist, a southern belle, a wealthy madam, a retired banker turned gambler, an orphaned boy and a travelling body-parts salesman all trade their various stories to pass the time.

Driving the carriage is one Zeke "the Freak" Sarandon, a retired soldier with more than one strange, nervous habit. Although he is an experienced traveller, and the only one insane enough to take the most direct route south, even he cannot prevent his passengers from each meeting their grisly demise, one by one.

Hot on the trail of the coach, astride an ancient mechanical horse blowing sparks and belching out toxic clouds of smoke, is a zombie gunslinger, the risen corpse of a murdered prospector.

For on the carriage is the one who killed him, and he must have his horrible, bloody revenge.

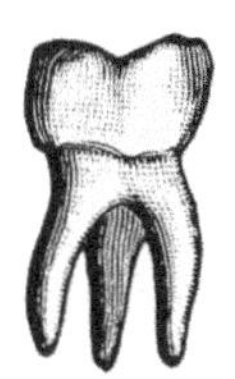

Bizarro Pulp Press
an imprint of JournalStone Publishing.

Published 2018

ISBN: 978-1-947654-40-2